SKULL CANYON

The deadly exploits of outlaw Zane Walker had grown more terrifying with every passing day. Nobody seemed able to catch the infamous rider, and those few who did get close were killed. Finally it fell to one man – Zane's identical twin brother Slim – to try to outwit the killer. As he trailed his brother over a hundred miles, Slim found that the land itself was even more dangerous than the rider he was hunting. Soon he would reach Skull Canyon, and it would have to end there – with knife or bullet...

SKULL CANYON

SKULL CANYON

by

Dean Edwards

Dales Large Print Books
Long Preston, North Yorkshire,
BD23 4ND, England.

British Library Cataloguing in Publication Data.

Edwards, Dean
    Skull Canyon.

    A catalogue record of this book is
    available from the British Library

    ISBN   1-84262-305-2 pbk

First published in Great Britain in 2003 by Robert Hale Ltd.

Published in Large Print 2004 by arrangement with
Robert Hale Ltd.

Dales Large Print is an imprint of Library Magna Books Ltd.

Printed and bound in Great Britain by
T.J. (International) Ltd., Cornwall, PL28 8RW

Dedicated to my godfather Michael Wall

PROLOGUE

It is said that a man is made up of two parts. The good and the evil. Most are capable of controlling their darker side whilst some find it impossible to do so. For the majority of humanity the unwritten rules of morality and respect for the law are abided by, but there have always been a few who seem either not to recognize those rules or who just choose to ignore them.

But most men were at least true to whichever dominant side of their personalities they favoured.

The greatest of men know that they had their evil personas under control; their evil counterparts knew that somewhere deep within their black hearts a spark of goodness somehow still glowed.

But that did nothing to explain the rarest of creatures who walked in human form and to all intents and purposes appeared to be perfectly normal: those cast from a single mould which was split into two halves before they had even been born, two entities that, although identical to look at, were in reality the complete opposite of one another.

One good and the other evil.

Men such as these were and are an oddity that even nature itself cannot explain, and yet they did and still do, exist.

Flesh and blood.

Apparently identical in every way on the outside and yet bearing no similarity to one another on the inside. One human being, cursed into two bodies. One blessed with all the good traits that make a man a man and the other cursed with nothing but absolute evil coursing through its veins.

What does the good man do when his evil twin is out of control? When he can no longer turn his back and ignore the atrocities that are left in the wake of the man who looks exactly the same as he himself?

Does he turn his back and walk away?

His entire nature prevents him from even considering that as an option. He cannot stand by and ignore what his other half is doing. For to do so would make him no better than his darker side.

One posse after another had ridden into the jaws of hell and been destroyed. Three sheriffs and twice as many deputies all suffered the same fate. Even a federal marshal could not match the sheer venom of the outlaw's deadly guns.

Could not stop him from riding on and on.

Everyone had failed because no one had any way of seeing into the mind of the man they pursued. They could not imagine what horrific depths his cruel imagination was capable of plunging into.

Year after year it had gone on unchecked.

Then, when all others had failed to locate his evil sibling, the one man who could do so, used his unique knowledge and attempted to stop his other half from continuing on his chosen path of destruction.

Even if it cost his own life, he had to try and stop his twin brother, because no one else could.

Yet, can the pure of heart accomplish such a feat without being destroyed themselves?

ONE

This was no ordinary rider who rode his black stallion out of the morning mist and headed straight for the unsuspecting Arizona township of Silver Springs. The streets were busy with all forms of beings and vehicles. Flatbed wagons rolled up and down the main street, to and from the General Feed Stores warehouse. Riders meandered in every direction. Men and women walked along the peaceful boardwalks without even giving the stranger in their midst a second glance.

For none of these people suspected a thing. To them he was just another drifting cowboy.

But they were wrong. This was a deadly killing machine who had never met anyone capable of even coming close to matching his gun skills.

Zane Walker had driven his powerful mount mercilessly, trying to get away from the rider who was hunting him, but knew in his black heart that it was an impossibility.

For the rider who trailed him was no bounty hunter or even another in the long line of lawmen who had chanced their luck.

The rider behind him was his self-righteous brother, Slim.

Zane Walker slowed the stallion's pace and eased the reins back as his eyes surveyed every face that innocently looked up at his own. They had no idea who he was or what he was capable of doing once the darkness came over him again.

Only his victims knew about that and most of them could not tell because they were dead.

Walker rubbed the grime from his face and looked over his shoulder at the dusty trail behind him. It had become a habit that he had no idea that he was doing any longer. For a hundred miles he had known that his twin brother was tracking him with the intention of capturing him and bringing him to justice.

Zane Walker knew how futile an enterprise that would be for even a skilled gunfighter to undertake. His brother hardly knew which end of a pistol the bullets came out of, let alone how to hit anything with one.

But Slim continued to follow him and was getting closer with every day that passed. If the two brothers had anything in common it was their dogged stubbornness.

The outlaw drew in his reins and stared at the Royal Flush saloon. He threw his leg over the neck of the stallion and slid down to the ground. People did not even look at him as he looped his reins over the hitching pole and then stepped up on to the boardwalk. Walker stared up and down the street and then across the wide thoroughfare.

His honed skills had already taken note of where the sheriff's office was. It looked the same as so many other law offices in so many other towns.

Zane Walker pulled the brim of his Stetson down, pushed the swing-doors open and entered the busy saloon. It was more than a month since he had last been anywhere so noisy. He aimed his battered boots in the direction of the bar and pushed aside all who got in his way.

He had a thirst on him that only hard liquor could cure.

The bartender watched the stranger with a lack of interest. He had seen so many faces across his wet counter over the years that they had all started to look exactly the same to his tired eyes.

'What ya want?' he asked loudly.

Zane Walker paused. He did not like the tone in the voice, yet he lowered his head and silently counted to five.

'Whiskey. A bottle.'

The bartender grunted.

'That'll cost ya two dollars.'

Walker stared at the palm of the man's hand and nodded as his fingers searched in his vest pocket for coins. He found two silver dollars and placed them on the open hand.

The bartender said nothing. He turned, and grabbed a black glass bottle from a shelf and placed it before the outlaw.

Walker studied the bottle with an educated eye. It was greasy and had no label. The cork was barely inside the long neck. The outlaw inhaled deeply and stood to his full height. He raised his head and allowed the man to see his angry eyes from beneath his wide hat-brim.

'I want a real bottle of whiskey, mister,' Walker said in a voice that was as cold as ice.

'That's what ya got,' the bartender said dismissively. 'Just drink it and don't start no trouble or I'll break a two-by-two across your skull. Understand?'

Zane Walker felt the eyes of everyone within earshot watching him as he pushed

15

the bottle back at the man.

'The dumb bastards who live in this town might not know what they're being served, but I do. Get me a bottle of whiskey with a label and an unbroken seal.'

'You talkin' to me, sonny?' The bartender slammed a fist on the bar-top and then reached beneath the long counter and grabbed hold of a pickaxe handle. It was a weapon that he had used more times than he could recall. Dried blood from all the previous heads it had cracked open stained its shaft.

The rest of the men at the bar moved away quickly. They had witnessed the bartender's fury before. As the man swung the four-foot long piece of wood around his head, his small beady eyes saw Zane Walker's left hand slap leather.

The Colt came out of the holster swiftly. Walker's thumb dragged the hammer back until it locked and then thrust the cold steel barrel into the face of the man.

'I'd stop if I was you,' the outlaw said in a hushed tone.

The bartender froze with the pickaxe handle in his hands above his head. He stared down the gun barrel straight at the face of the outlaw. There was no sign of humanity in Walker's features. The man knew that this was no bluff.

The finger on the trigger wanted to squeeze it.

'Who the hell are ya, mister?' the bartender asked. Slowly he lowered his wooden weapon until it rested on the counter of the bar.

'Zane Walker.'

The room went even quieter than it had been when the saloon's patrons had seen the pistol being pushed into the face of the angry bartender.

The man's face began to twitch. He suddenly realized how close he had come to being killed in cold blood.

'I'm sorry, Zane. I had no idea it was you.'

Walker pulled the trigger.

The Royal Flush echoed with the sound of the deadly bullet as it passed through the bartender's head and shattered the large mirror behind him.

If it were possible for people to stampede, then that was what those inside the saloon did. By the time the body crumpled on to the blood-soaked floor, Walker was standing alone beside the long wooden counter.

'Nobody calls me Zane unless I give 'em permission,' Walker said. He lifted the bar-flap and stepped over the body. His boots stuck to the sticky floor as he walked through the gore and glass until he found an expensive bottle of whiskey.

The ruthless outlaw rested his pistol on top of the bar-top, pulled the cork from the bottle, then poured three fingers of the amber liquor into a glass tumbler. As he held the glass, the outlaw saw the two men standing in the doorway.

Walker lifted the glass to his lips and swallowed the entire measure of whiskey in one go. Then he lowered it back to the bar and rested it on the wet surface.

The stars on their shirts made it obvious what they were. The scatterguns in their hands made it clear what they intended to do.

'Stay exactly where you are, Walker,' the larger man said as he walked across the sawdust-covered floor towards the outlaw.

'You know who I am?' Walker smiled. 'News sure travels fast in this town, Sheriff.'

The second man advanced towards the bar-counter. He too held his scattergun across his waist his index finger resting on the triggers.

Both lawmen trained their weapons on Walker. They were nervous and it showed.

'Give it up, son. One move and we'll blast

you into a million pieces,' the sheriff added.

Zane Walker lowered his chin until it touched the knot in his bandanna. His eyes burned furiously at the pair.

'I'd quit while you're ahead, boys.'

It was a vain warning. These men knew little except how to pull the triggers on their scatterguns. They upheld the law whenever they were called upon to do so. For the entire time that they had held office, they had never had to deal with anything more difficult than Saturday-night drunks. They continued to move towards the outlaw because they could see that his pistol was lying on top of the wet bar next to the whiskey bottle.

'Get them hands up in the air, Walker,' the sheriff screamed at the narrow-eyed man.

Zane Walker knew that these men only had slightly to tease the triggers on their double-barrelled shotguns to blast him and half the saloon wall away, but he still would not do as they commanded.

It was not his way.

'I suggest you put them guns down and hightail it out of here,' Walker said. He poured another three fingers of whiskey into the glass tumbler before him. 'I'll kill you both for sure if you don't.'

The deputy glanced across at the sheriff.

'I ain't hankering to get myself killed, Jonas.'

The sheriff laughed gruffly and pointed his barrel at the bottle in Walker's hand.

'Even Jesse James couldn't pick up a gun and fire it with a bottle of rye in his hand, Bobby.'

With the speed that defied the human eye to see, Walker's left hand scooped the Colt off the bar-top, cocked and fired twice before twirling the still-smoking weapon back into his holster.

The two lawmen were both hit dead-centre and fell backwards into the sawdust. The scatterguns blasted into the saloon ceiling as the men's lifeless bodies hit the floor.

Zane Walker swallowed the drink.

'Jesse James ain't left-handed, you dumb bastard.'

TWO

The swirling sand cut through the hot air and tormented the eyes of the rider and defied him to see his distant prey. But he knew the man he hunted was out there somewhere, hiding or just waiting for one clear shot at his determined follower. Every bone in the rider's body told him so.

The horseman spat the sand from his mouth and then rubbed the sharp granules out of his eyes. He vowed that he was not about to stop trailing this man however unpleasant it became to do so.

There comes a time when a wise man knows when to quit. The problem with wisdom is that it is something that has to be learned and cannot be taken for granted.

Slim Walker stepped from his saddle on to the sun-baked ground and swallowed hard when the true magnitude of his situation dawned on his tired mind. The chase had now taken an entirely new turn. Now he was not simply trailing a man across vast fertile ranges but was confronted by a totally alien landscape, of which he had no experience.

He had ridden for nearly a hundred miles trailing the ruthless outlaw and knew that now the stakes had been upped to a point that verged on life and death. The problem was that Walker was not prepared for this new terrain.

He had insufficient provisions and was low on water.

Walker rested an arm on the neck of his exhausted horse and sighed heavily. He wondered who was the most tired, the animal or he himself. The annoying breeze that had kicked sand into his eyes and mouth for the previous hour suddenly stopped as quickly as it had started.

Even though he had been unable to see very far ahead for the last hour as he carefully followed the tracks in the sand, he had noticed that the temperature was rising steadily. Now it was like standing next to a bonfire. His skin burned even though covered by clothing.

As Walker managed to clear his eyes of the last of the blinding sand he felt his heart pounding. The sight before him was totally unexpected.

He was worried.

Slim Walker had lived all his life in Arizona

but had never been to this place before. The landscape was impressive but it terrified him. This place seemed to fit every description he had ever heard about Hell.

But he knew that this was not Hell. You had to be dead to get a glimpse of that place and he hurt too much to be anything but still very much alive.

He rubbed his rump and then attempted to pull his sweat-soaked denim pants away from his sore inner thighs. He had ridden hard and had the scars to prove it.

Walker glanced up and tried to remain calm as he looked at the view that filled his entire line of sight.

Magnificent purple mesas rose from the sun-baked prairie floor and touched the clouds above his head. The almost-red sand was interrupted by sparse patches of green sagebrush that somehow defied the blistering heat and clung to life. The rider looked up through his sand-filled eyebrows at the sky above him. It was a dangerous sky filled with clouds of every hue. Rumbling thunder echoed all around the vast valleys that faced him. Yet there was no sign of it raining anywhere near him.

There was no sign of anything else living in the valleys, which seemed to roll on into infinity. Slim Walker unscrewed the stopper on his canteen, then dropped his hat between the forelegs of the lathered-up horse and poured half its contents into it.

This was the last of the three canteens of water. It had been two days since he had found anything remotely resembling a waterhole. He wondered if the outlaw had deliberately led him away from the areas of precious liquid.

The horse drank and Walker took one small sip before returning the canteen to the saddle horn. It hung next to the pair of empty ones. He had only the water that remained in his canteen left and could not see anything out there ahead of him that looked as if it might provide him with any more.

This was indeed an unholy place.

A place that only fools willingly entered into without plenty of water and food. Yet Walker did not have enough of either, for he had not realized where he was being led. He had blindly followed his prey to a land that was totally treacherous. Once again the fox had proved that he had the hound exactly where he wanted him.

There seemed to be nothing out there that remotely resembled anything he had ever set eyes upon before. Death seemed to be out there mocking the rider, laughing at his reluctance to face his own fears.

Slim Walker knew that he had to continue yet every sinew in his body was screaming out for him to yield to his own instincts and give up his quest.

But that was impossible.

He had to continue to follow the tracks that were before him in the soft red sand. He alone could catch the rider who was out there somewhere ahead of him in the shimmering heat haze. Slim Walker knew that there were a thousand and one places his quarry might be lying in wait for him.

Waiting to bushwhack him.

Yet however deadly the outlaw was, he did not frighten Slim Walker. For he knew him almost as well as he knew himself.

Walker knew that he was out of his depth just trailing the outlaw. This was something he had never done before. To trail a wanted killer as if he were tracking an animal was against everything he held dear, yet it was his duty to do so.

He alone could find this outlaw, for only he knew how the evil man thought. For he was part of the same coin. A coin which had been split in two long ago.

The man whom he had trailed for the last hundred miles was his own twin brother, younger than himself by almost an hour. They had been described as identical for over fifteen years until the truth became evident to all who knew them both. For Slim and his brother Zane had been the ultimate twin brothers. Total opposites of one another.

Slim had been good and Zane evil. It was as simple as that.

Neither man totally a whole person but extremes of one man betrayed by nature itself in their mother's womb. Somehow torn into two by fate.

A mockery of what their Maker had intended.

Slim Walker was no bounty hunter and had seldom used the gun he wore, unlike his sharp-shooting sibling. Yet now he was on the trail of Zane with only one thought in his head.

He had to put an end to the evil.

Zane Walker had to be stopped from continuing his killing by the only man capable of doing so.

No lawman had ever managed to get close to the outlaw but Slim Walker instinctively knew how his brother thought and what he was doing. Since childhood Slim's mind had been haunted by all the atrocities his brother had committed.

At first he had thought them just childish nightmares until the truth had dawned upon his innocent mind. He had somehow been able to see the sickening rampage Zane Walker was inflicting through his own brother's eyes. Even now, Slim knew what Zane was planning.

Zane was out there waiting to kill him, as he had killed so many others over the years. There was no animosity in it, just a cold-blooded resolve. He killed because he could. It was the one thing at which he had always excelled. Yet Zane Walker had one weakness and that was his inability to stop his brother from seeing into his very thoughts, from knowing what his next move would be and then acting on the secret information.

Staring out into the heat, Slim Walker tried to work out why his brother had led him to this place.

Was it by accident?

He doubted that.

Or was it because he wanted to lure his follower into a land that he was not prepared for? A land that would kill him for making the mistake of entering its deadly

27

boundaries. This was a merciless place which burned at the skin as well as the souls of men who dared enter into it.

Slim Walker plucked his Stetson up from the ground, placed it on his head and then gathered up the reins from the red sand. It was an easy trail to follow. Zane Walker had made no attempt to try and hide his tracks from his brother.

He wanted him to follow and die.

For a hundred miles Zane had reeled Slim in like a trout on the end of a fishing-line.

Slim stepped into his stirrup, mounted the tired horse and jabbed his spurs into the flesh of the animal. He knew that he could stay alive if he just kept seeing through Zane's eyes.

For the first time in his life he prayed that the visions would continue.

The horse walked across the red sand and its rider teased the reins as his eyes surveyed everything before him. Yet he knew that even if his brother did not claim his life, the land itself just might.

THREE

Twenty days earlier an apprehensive Slim Walker had ridden into the seemingly quiet town of Silver Springs. He should have known better than to think the townspeople would forget his face so quickly. Yet it had not been his face they recalled but the mirror image sported by his brother Zane that frightened them.

The horseman teased the mount down the centre of the main street. With every stride of the horse's long legs Walker looked to either side of him at the terror etched into the features of the town's citizens. He wondered how his brother could manage to create such fear. Such hatred.

He had allowed his horse to find its own pace along the wide main street and had noticed that women were dragging their children into their homes at just the sight of him. It seemed strange to the rider that Zane could have caused such feelings in decent folks. Slim felt ashamed to have the same blood flowing through his veins. At the

29

end of the long street he spied the sign that his bones had longed to see for days.

The rider turned the head of his mount to the front of the building before coming to a stop outside the small clean hotel.

A thousand whispers had filled his ears.

Slim Walker dismounted and tied his reins to the hitching pole directly outside the colourful glass window. He untied his saddle-bags and tossed them over his shoulder. He stepped up on to the boardwalk knowing that he was now probably a target for those who thought him to be his brother.

Walker had hesitated outside the open doorway of the hotel and begun to think about the countless dozens of faces he had encountered upon entering Silver Springs. He should have become aware that things were not right sooner but he was dog-tired.

If he had been of a darker nature, like his brother, he would have become enraged that all the people whom he had silently greeted with a touch of his hat-brim had shown him nothing but contempt and fear.

But Slim Walker felt only regret.

The faces of those brave enough to continue standing on the boardwalks were like stone. Their screwed-up eyes were all aimed at the tall handsome figure who had made a vain attempt to brush the trail grime from his sun-bleached clothing.

Walker licked his dry, cracked lips and entered the hotel's cool interior. The hot sun could not touch the foyer of this place. The coolness came as a welcome relief to his sun-baked body as he walked across the lobby to the small desk. A tall female stood behind the counter and seemed to freeze to the spot when her eyes recognized the handsome face.

Harriet Cole knew what it was like to be physically taken by the man who stood before her. Her long fingers traced at the front of her dress and recalled how she had been just one of the many women Zane Walker had used. Yet unlike any of the others, she had almost welcomed the attention. For her marriage had long been nothing more than a sham. A masquerade like so many others within the small town.

Had he returned to continue what he had started? Her mind raced with a multitude of unanswered questions. She found beads of sweat trickling down from her neck and rolling over her ample bosoms before disappearing into her cleavage.

Then Harriet Cole noticed that the so-familiar eyes, which she thought she

31

recognized, did not show any interest in her low-cut dress or its contents.

She was confused.

Only a few days earlier this man had carried her up the stairs over his shoulder and torn her clothing from her willing body and made love to her. Now he seemed totally unaware of what, for her, was an unforgettable moment in her otherwise boring existence. Had there been so many conquests in the outlaw's life that Zane Walker could not even remember her?

Harriet Cole had said nothing when the tall man approached her desk. She wanted to throw herself into his arms and beg for more but knew that her husband Jonathan was in the next room. She tapped the loud bell with the palm of her small hand continuously until the large figure of Jonathan Cole appeared from the neat dining-room.

The overweight man sported long un-checked side-whiskers that did nothing to enhance his features.

Slim Walker noticed her eyes darting across the room to the man, who suddenly slowed his pace until he reached the side of his blushing wife and leaned nervously on the desk.

Jonathan Cole was a man who looked as if

he could tear the head off a grizzly bear, but faced with Walker, he seemed totally impassive.

It was something that the rider had experienced in more than ten towns since he had started out on his quest to find his twin brother. Whatever evil Zane Walker had done to these people was probably far worse than his innocent mind could ever imagine.

Slim Walker felt as if he ought to be continually apologizing for whatever Zane had put them through, but after riding into the third town he had decided not to open his mouth unless challenged by someone.

'What can we do for ya?' Jonathan Cole asked.

'I'd like a room,' Slim replied.

'The same one as last time?'

'I've never been here before, mister.'

The woman moved behind her husband and allowed him to deal with Walker. She could not take her curious eyes off the man whom she felt she knew better than her own husband. He claimed that he had never been here before and yet she knew better. Had he lost his memory?

Jonathan Cole stared hard at the man who signed the register with his right hand.

'Why have you returned, Mr Walker?'

Slim Walker tilted his head and stared knowingly into the troubled face. He knew that it had taken more than a little courage to say those words.

'I ain't Zane Walker, mister. I'm his brother Slim.'

The two people behind the hotel desk looked at one another before returning their confused gaze upon the tall man before them. Once again, Slim Walker recognized the look.

'You say that you ain't Zane Walker?' the man nervously asked.

Walker nodded.

'Nope. But he's the reason that I'm here, *amigo*.'

The female suddenly seemed to melt; she moved back to her place behind the small counter. Harriet Cole leaned on the hotel register and fluttered her long eyelashes at him. Now she understood. Zane Walker had used his left hand to draw his gun and write his name. This man wore his gun on his right hip and held the pen with his right hand. But even knowing that he was not the man who had made passionate love to her seemed hard to totally accept.

'You're the spittin' image of that brother of yours.' She sighed heavily. How much like his brother was he? The thought lingered in her mind as she studied him carefully.

'I know. It can be kinda dangerous to a man's health looking so much like Zane.' Walker removed his Stetson and hung it on the grip of his gun. 'I've had three men shoot at me in the last month.'

'Your brother is an evil bastard,' Jonathan Cole said.

'I know,' Walker agreed.

The female heaved her ample bosom.

'You say that your brother brings you to Silver Springs?'

'Yes, ma'am. I'm trying to catch up with Zane,' Slim Walker replied.

'You ain't in the same line of work, are you?' Cole asked clearing his throat and removing a room-key from the line of numbered hooks behind him.

Walker shook his head.

'Nope. I'm trying to catch Zane and bring him to justice.'

The couple glanced at one another again.

'Are you saying that you're gonna risk your life and try and capture him?' the man stammered as he thought about the prospect of trying to get the better of the ruthless outlaw.

'Yep.' Slim Walker nodded.

'You must either be mighty brave or real stupid.' The female smiled. 'Which is it?'

'A little of both.' Slim Walker held out his hand for the key but Harriet Cole plucked it from her husband's fingers, strolled around the desk and headed towards the staircase.

'I'll show Mr Walker to his room, Jonathan. You rustle up some food for our guests. It's almost lunch-time.'

Slim Walker nodded to the burly man and then trailed the woman to the staircase. His eyes watched as her bustle rocked with the movement of her hips. Coyly he followed Harriet Cole up to the second floor.

The corridor was darker than the rest of the hotel due to the fact that the blind was pulled down on the only window facing the street.

'It's kinda dark up here, ain't it?' Walker asked innocently.

She paused just long enough for him to bump into her.

'The sun tends to take all the colour out of the carpeting, Mr Walker.'

Slim Walker stopped when he saw her slipping the key into the lock and turning it gently. She turned the handle and pushed the door open. Harriet Cole floated across the room with the tired man close behind her.

His eyes looked at the welcoming bed bathed in sunlight when she raised the blind from the window.

Slim Walker dropped his saddle-bags on top of the white bed-linen and then felt her body pressing into his. He stared down into her face and felt himself gulp when he saw the passion in her eyes.

He did not understand.

'Your brother made love to me,' she said, wrapping her arms around his waist. 'He tore at my dress and then my underthings and then drove himself into me.'

'I'm sorry, ma'am,' Slim apologized.

Harriet Cole's face looked straight at his. 'Don't be sorry. He was wonderful. Just as I think you too could be. You being so much like him, and all.'

Walker felt her hands all over him. He had never had much luck with females and was shocked when her fingers began to unbuckle his belt. Nervously he backed straight into a wall but there was no escape from her. She clung to his lean frame like fresh paint and continued to tear feverishly at his clothing.

Slim's eyes widened. 'Do you think that maybe you ought not to be doing this, ma'am?'

'My name's Harriet,' she managed to say

as her lips traced all over his dust-caked skin.

'Harriet? Right.' Walker felt his heart pounding faster and faster as blood sought places it had seldom gone before. Places that made it difficult not to notice.

'You even taste like him.' Harriet Cole informed the startled man.

'Your father might hear us, ma'am.' Slim Walker tried to protest but he had had little practice at doing even this. She had forgotten more than he had ever learned concerning such matters.

Harriet dragged his head down and kissed his sore lips, then released him long enough for him to get air into his lungs. He felt his shirt being torn open and then her right hand slipping down into his pants.

'He's not my father. He's my husband. But don't pay him no heed.' Her words came quickly. Breathlessly.

Walker tried to push her away but she was far stronger than he had imagined.

'But I don't want to upset a married man.'

'Why not? He's been upsetting me for years.'

'How?'

'He keeps waking up every morning,' she cooed. 'You can't imagine how upsetting that can be to a woman who has her heart set on widowhood.'

Slim Walker felt her getting more and more excited. She was married OK, he thought. No single lady could be that experienced. Then, when she knew that she had his full attention, she withdrew one hand and grabbed at his jacket.

She pulled him away from the wall and bit at the hairs on his exposed chest. Before he could make a sound she gave a mighty heave and threw him.

Slim Walker felt himself falling sideways.

Walker landed on the well-sprung mattress and bounced up and down. He lay helplessly on his back watching as she closed the door and then placed the key in its lock.

The sound of the key being turned filled his ears.

'So I guess this means that you kinda liked Zane,' Slim heard himself say.

'I will show you how much I like Zane.'

Slowly she unbuttoned her bodice.

FOUR

The blazing sun seemed to ignore the thick denim jacket on Slim Walker's back and burned straight through to his skin. The rider pulled a bandanna from his hip pocket and wrapped it around his neck in a vain attempt to stop the merciless rays from frying his skin like bacon. Even when he turned the collar of his jacket up and adjusted his Stetson, Walker could still feel the intense heat torturing him.

He had been riding for less than thirty minutes since the sand storm had ended but it felt more like a week. The horse was walking over the red sand slowly but the rider knew that this was insanity. The further he ventured into this place, the hotter it became.

The sound of thunder rippled around the high mesas and made both horse and rider nervous. Walker did not want to get caught out in the open should lightning start to fork down from the heavens. He had seen what a bolt of lightning could do to a man and horse before, and did not wish to have it happen to him.

Slim held on to his reins tightly and tried to work out where he might seek cover in the unforgiving land. The nearest of the mesas was miles away, although it was impossible to gauge distance accurately out on the red sand.

Walker's eyes looked up at the clouds above him. White, pink and black. All moving at different speeds in various directions. They too made it difficult to estimate where the safest place in this valley might be. He teased the horse to increase its pace as his mind raced.

The horse began to kick up sand from its hoofs. Walker stood in his stirrups and leaned forward, trying to take the weight off the poor animal's back.

The tracks of his brother's horse appeared to head straight through the middle of the wide valley and disappear off into the distance.

Slim knew that must be where Zane wanted him to head. For once he realized that he did not have to blindly follow those tracks but could head off towards one of the immense natural towers. There was a chance that he might even find pockets of water nearer the rocks than out in the centre of this blistering desert of taunting scarlet sand.

Slowly, Slim Walker eased his reins to his left and guided the cantering mount towards the base of the nearest mesa.

Had he finally outwitted his brother? Had he managed to do the exact opposite of what Zane wanted him to do?

The sound of a distant rifle shot resounded off the high mesa walls a fraction of a second after blood burst from the neck of his horse. It was a gruesome wound. Slim Walker had just managed to see the bullet passing through the neck of the animal as it began to fall.

Somehow he managed to throw himself clear of the dead weight as the animal crashed into the red sand.

Slim rolled over several times before coming to a halt beside a clump of sagebrush. He stared at the dead horse in shock and then heard another shot. He heard the bullet passing through the air above his head.

He scrambled to the side of the stricken animal and lay against the saddle. More bullets hit the dead horse, making it jolt with their impact.

Slim Walker dragged the canteens off the saddle horn and held them close to his chest.

For the first time since he had started out after his brother, he knew what fear felt like.

FIVE

'So you really thought that you could get the better of me, did ya, brother Slim?' Zane Walker smiled through the gunsmoke that trailed from the end of his Winchester barrel. 'I'd rather see you dead than let you keep on hounding my damn trail.'

He pulled the trigger again and sent another well-aimed bullet over the flat valley floor at the fallen horse. His brother did not return fire. Zane Walker knew that Slim had gone down heavily when he had opened up with his carbine. Any one of the half-dozen rifle shots could have hit the inexperienced rider as the horse had started to fall, but the only way to make sure was to go and find Slim's body.

Zane Walker pushed the lever of his Winchester down and felt the hot shell casing pass by his cheek. The outlaw stood up from the hot red sand and stared hard out at the distance and the fallen horse.

For the first time in his life, the outlaw felt uneasy about venturing back to one of his victims. There was not an ounce of guilt in his having bushwhacked yet another innocent person with his long rifle, but something held him back from inspecting his handiwork. Perhaps it was the thought of seeing someone who looked exactly like himself dead on the red sand that chilled the ruthless outlaw. If Zane looked down on the body of Slim, it would be as if he were seeing himself.

Zane spat at the sand, then he returned to the black stallion and slid the barrel of the carbine into the saddle scabbard. As far as he was concerned it was now over. Even if Slim was still alive it did not matter. He had lured his brother into the wasteland and killed his mount, knowing that without a horse he was as good as dead anyway.

This was a land that took no prisoners.

Zane stepped into his stirrup, grabbed hold of the saddle horn and pulled himself on to the back of the big animal. He pushed the toe of his right boot into the other stirrup and then hauled his reins hard until the stallion turned around.

A nagging thought kept gnawing at his mind. What if Slim was neither dead nor injured? What if he was still able to continue following on after his evil twin? Zane Walker spat at the sand again and stared out at the arid landscape before him.

He had to make speed now and reach his destination. Only he knew of the natural hideout that lay deep in the heart of this god-forsaken place.

He jabbed his spurs into the flesh of the mount and rode further into the unforgiving land. He knew where he was going and how to get there.

The outlaw galloped off through the soft red sand, using his long reins like a whip. He knew where to find water and that was all that mattered.

Zane Walker drove the faithful horse straight down the centre of the wide valley between the towering mesas at a speed that few others could have equalled.

Zane Walker's mind drifted back to the dead horse. He had no idea whether any of his bullets had hit his twin brother. But he did not give a damn.

Anyone on foot in this hot deadly place was doomed. If he had hit Slim with any of his rifle shots it was probably an act of mercy.

For fresh warm blood would bring the wolves down from the mesas and the vultures off the high thermals. They would make short work of any man or beast wounded in the blistering hot valley.

Zane Walker rode into the heat haze and disappeared.

He was heading to the only place that he knew would protect him. He was headed for Skull Canyon.

The hunter had suddenly become the hunted. Slim Walker crawled to the side of his dead horse and stared down the long valley, expecting to see his brother moving in on him with his deadly rifle.

Zane, unlike Slim, knew how to finish off his prey. A trail of bodies bore testament to that fact. They had littered the route for more than a hundred miles to this sun-baked land.

Slim saw the rising dust away in the distance and knew that Zane was not riding towards him. He was heading away.

The winded man staggered to his feet and watched the distant dust falling to the ground slowly on the hot air. The heat haze made it impossible for his eyes to focus.

He turned and gazed down to his side. The sight of the bullet-ridden body of his horse beside him turned his guts. It had never been a mount that could equal his brother's magnificent stallion but it had always been a loyal beast. The horse had cost just fifty dollars, with the saddle thrown in, and was already past its best even then, but it had never faltered.

It had ridden its heart out trying to catch up with the thoroughbred stallion. It had come damn close to catching it, the dust-caked man thought.

It had taken bullets to stop its relentless progress.

Slim Walker kicked at the red sand and shook his head in despair. His keen eyes flashed all around at the land which surrounded him and the high mesas that loomed above him. Even now there was no sign of any other living thing.

Zane had left him for dead.

His own flesh and blood had thrown him to the buzzards.

Suddenly he knew that every story that he had ever heard about his evil sibling was true. He had doubted some of the things that had been attributed to Zane during the last hundred or so miles, until now. But anyone who could shoot the horse out from under his own brother and then leave him for the vultures to pick clean was no good.

For a few fleeting seconds he thought that

maybe there still remained a spark of humanity in his brother's soul, otherwise Zane would have killed him. Then Slim knew the truth. Zane had not been aiming at the horse at all.

He had been trying to shoot him and only the shimmering heat haze had caused Zane's aim to falter.

Slim hung the empty canteens over his shoulder and then felt the half-full one. He had been saving it for the horse, but now the sad creature would never be thirsty again. He unscrewed its stopper and downed its entire contents.

It was the first decent drink that he had had for days. He hung the third empty canteen over his shoulder with the others and then untied the bags from behind the saddle cantle and hung them over his other shoulder.

He continued to walk to the high mesa that had been his goal before his brother had shot the horse from beneath him. He had enough dried beef jerky to last him three days in his saddle-bags, and a box of bullets for the gun on his hip.

A gun that he had never even fired.

As Slim Walker made his way through the soft sand he knew that all he needed was

49

water. The sky continued to rumble over his head but not a single raindrop fell from the moody clouds.

With every step, he felt the sun burning into him.

SIX

The news of an outlaw with $5,000 on his head, travelling deep into the heart of Arizona, had already spread along the telegraph wires before Zane Walker had even left Silver Springs. Had it been any other infamous gunman roaming towards them, there would have been dozens of peace officers heading out for the tempting reward money already.

But Zane Walker was no ordinary outlaw. He was known for his totally ruthless attitude to anyone who got in his way. His was the worst kind of reputation that a man could have, but he had earned every bit of it. The blood of one victim had barely dried before he had claimed another.

The grim information of Walker's impending arrival in some of the major Arizona towns and cities had reached the thriving Tombstone first. From there the vivid details were sent out to all the smaller towns fortunate enough to have a telegraph office. Those not connected to the talking wires

51

would have to face the heartless outlaw in total ignorance.

Broken Gulch was a town that had a well-equipped telegraph office but little else remotely connected with civilization. A settlement made up entirely of adobe structures, for no trees grew in this harsh place, Broken Gulch survived on the very edge of the land of towering mesas.

How it survived was a miracle in itself. Yet for more than a generation the small dwellings made from the red sand that surrounded it, had done so.

Its lawmen were no better or worse than any of the others within a hundred square miles of the arid landscape to the west, but they had one advantage over all the other Arizona towns seeking to capture Zane Walker.

They were closer to the desolate valleys and high mesas than all the rest. Yet the peace officers who kept control of the quiet township of Broken Gulch were far from being mere inexperienced tax-collectors, like some of their colleagues in the more prosperous towns to the east and north.

The sheriff and his deputy knew exactly how to use their arsenal of various weaponry, and often did so, even if they had to venture far away from the remote adobe settlement.

Sheriff Marvin Peabody had earned his star the hard way after a lifetime of being a hired gunfighter skimming the law by the skin of his teeth. Men like Peabody were a rarity this far west and were getting rarer as more and more outlaws ventured into the territory. His deputy, Tom Smith was half his age and twice the shot of his mentor. What he lacked in experience, he made up for in sheer enthusiasm.

Neither could have survived on their meagre salaries and both knew how to add to their income. Both men roamed far beyond the boundaries of the thirty-building town and were known for their straight shooting and tendency not to waste taxpayers' money by bringing in their prisoners alive.

If the Wanted posters said Dead or Alive, they tried to avoid the latter.

No man deserved to live if he had managed to get his name and likeness on a Wanted poster, Sheriff Peabody had said many times over the years.

Dead meant dead.

There was no middle way.

For nearly three weeks they had known

that the notorious Zane Walker was in their vicinity, getting closer with every heartbeat. The two lawmen had agreed that they would split the bounty straight down the middle if the outlaw came anywhere near Broken Gulch. But they had waited too long for Walker to get to them and had decided that the only way they could ensure realizing the Federal bounty money was to seek him out, and then kill him.

They had no fear of any outlaws. They had killed enough of them to know that they were nothing more than vermin. And you destroyed vermin without a second thought.

It seemed a sure bet that Zane Walker would head to their town as it was the closest to the unnamed deadly valley into which he had been last reported entering. But it did not take that length of time to negotiate the blazing hot valleys.

Sheriff Peabody knew that there were a hundred or more places where an army could hide out down there amid the towering mesas.

The two lawmen had spent three hours preparing their horses and pack-mule for their latest deadly expedition. This was not something either man wanted to rush. It had to be done properly. They had to have enough water and food for themselves and their animals to survive in the unholy landscape to the west of Broken Gulch.

One miscalculation could prove fatal.

They knew that the outlaw was heading through the deadly valleys toward them. But he was ordinary gunslinger and had survived his bloody rampage because he was smart.

Only a smart man could or would use that place for a hideout.

Only a man who knew the lethal terrain well would even dare trying to use it as a short cut or sanctuary.

They knew that Zane Walker had been reported several times over the previous few years as being in or around the blistering valley of mesas. Peabody now felt sure he knew why. It was the only thing that made any sense.

The sheriff chewed on his plug of tobacco and watched his deputy finishing tying everything down on the ill-tempered mule.

'This Walker critter must have himself a hideout down there in them crags or someplace, Tom.' The older lawman spat a lump of black goo to end his sentence.

'I heard tell that there are caves down there, Sheriff,' Tom Smith said as he fashioned a knot in the rope under the mule's girth.

Peabody nodded and spat another lump of black spittle at the ground between them.

'Yep. There are plenty of caves down there OK. I found a few of the things years back.'

'We going to search 'em?' Smith's face seemed eager to the point of excitement.

'Reckon so, young 'un.'

'But how could a man survive down there? I thought there weren't no water down in the valley.' Tom Smith brooded thoughtfully as he walked around the animals inspecting his handiwork.

The sheriff raised one of his bushy eyebrows. 'There's water down there if'n ya know where to look, Tom.'

'Do you know where to look, Sheriff?' Smith was not sure that they had enough water packed on their mounts and the mule. This was no ordinary place they were going to ride into. He was used to the vast prairies and deserts that made up most of Arizona's terrain but knew nothing about the valleys of high rocky peaks.

The older man spat once more. 'Yep. Reckon I do.'

'Then we'll be OK?' Smith's face sought an answer. For the first time since he had become a deputy he was unsure that they were doing the right thing.

'Right as rain, *amigo.*' Peabody grinned, allowing his tobacco-stained teeth to be seen. It was not a pleasant sight.

'Who is this Walker varmint, anyway?' The deputy stepped closer to the sheriff who stood on the boardwalk outside their office.

The sheriff pulled the Wanted poster from his pants pocket and unfolded it carefully.

'He's a killer. Robs anyone who gets in his way and just kills 'em.'

Smith glanced at the crude photographic image on the creased paper. 'How many men does it say he has killed?'

'It says that he's killed ten here but I had me a wire last week that said he done for five folks in Silver Springs about a month back.' The sheriff spat again. 'Kinda mean bastard by all accounts.'

'And he's worth five thousand dollars.' Smith smiled wide.

Peabody refolded the poster and pushed it down into his pocket.

'That'll buy us a damn good time, and no mistake.' The sheriff stretched his arms and looked at the low sun. Few men liked to hit the trail after sundown, but Peabody preferred to ride in the cooler air beneath a million stars.

'Is there a moon tonight, Sheriff?'

'Yep. A nice juicy yella one,' Peabody replied, staring up at the sky with a knowing eye.

'We gonna need all these rifles and ammunition?' Smith queried. 'He's just one man.'

'The buffalo gun might not be required but ya never know.' The sheriff winked and stepped down from the raised boardwalk.

The deputy looked straight at the face of the lawman. 'Are you scared, Sheriff?'

Sheriff Peabody spat at the ground again.

'Yep. Only a fool or madman never gets scared, Tom.'

SEVEN

The temperature had fallen noticeably within minutes of the sun's dropping beneath the high peaks above the floor of the mysterious valleys. But that offered no comfort to the exhausted Slim Walker as he continued to stagger through the soft red sand. He regretted drinking all his water in one go and was now starting to think that he might never find any more.

This was a land of total opposites.

The merciless rays of the sun had been replaced by bone-chilling coldness. Walker staggered and fell to his knees and stared around the moonlit valley. Now everything appeared to be bathed in a soft blue light. Mist was starting to rise off the sand and it troubled him. With every passing minute, his field of vision was being eroded.

Slim had been walking for nearly two hours since leaving the body of his horse. He refused to stop searching for a place where he might locate enough water to fill his empty canteens.

It had proved a vain quest so far.

If there was water in this unholy land, it was well hidden.

Walker breathed heavily as exhaustion overwhelmed his lean frame. He had never felt so desperate before. His burning eyes stared at his own breath leaving his mouth and nostrils, and made him wonder exactly how cold it was going to get before sunrise.

If he survived that long.

Somehow Slim Walker managed to haul himself back on to his feet. He paused for a few moments. He looked down at his boots and knew they were perfect for riding but were hindering his progress over the soft surface of the valley floor. Yet there was no way he could find the strength to remove and carry them on his journey.

Inhaling deeply, Walker started striding once more in the direction that he knew his brother had taken. Even now he still believed he had to pursue his bloodthirsty sibling. It was his duty.

The empty canteens bounced off his hip and the saddle-bag satchels beat a rhythm on his back and belly, but he staggered on and on through the sand. He was following his chosen course by using the foot of the high mesa as a rough guide.

The change in the temperature had happened so swiftly that the beads of sweat on his face had frozen to his burned skin.

He was tired. All he wanted to do was lie on the sand, close his eyes and allow sleep to envelop him. But fear kept him upright and heading towards his unknown destination. For to succumb to his exhaustion and fall asleep would be to allow death to claim him.

Even with his jacket buttoned to his chin, the intense cold began to reach into the marrow of his bones. Every step had become a torturous reminder of his ordeal.

But he continued walking.

Step after step he forced himself forward against the screams of every sinew in his aching body. Somehow Walker managed to cover another quarter-mile before he heard the sound of rumbling again. He looked up at the sky expecting to see storm clouds but there were none.

Countless stars and a large moon mocked him.

Was he going insane?

It might have been the lack of water playing tricks on his weary brain or just the cold night air freezing his every lucid thought.

Whatever it was, it sounded like thunder.

But was this reality or just another part of a vivid hallucination haunting him? Slim shook his head and tried to regain his senses.

The sound was still out there, he thought. It was real!

Slim Walker felt his knees buckle beneath him before he toppled on to his face. The taste of sand in his dry mouth made him angry. He craved sleep but had already wandered into his own personal nightmare. Once more his dogged determination refused to yield to his own weariness.

Slim clawed his way up off the sand using the mesa's rocky foundations as support. During the blisteringly hot day, the heat haze had mocked his vision, making it impossible to focus on anything clearly. Now the cold night air was dragging the trapped heat out of the red sand all around him. A mist swirled about the surface of the valley floor, making it increasingly hard to see anything except the towers of rock that reached up to the heavens.

How could Zane have done this to him? his mind asked over and over again.

A glancing light temporarily blinded the young man. He tried vainly to work out what it was but he could not see through the mist. Then it happened again.

Something was catching the reflected light of the bright moon high above him. Slim raised his right hand to shield his eyes from the flashing light that cut through the mist every few seconds.

Then he heard the rumbling noise once again. This time he knew that it was not thunder coming from above, but the sound of something heading directly towards him.

He gritted his teeth and wondered what could be out here in this unknown land.

Slim Walker kept his hand in front of his eyes. He was desperate to see what was moving straight at him. His mind raced as he began to imagine all sorts of things.

Had his brother Zane decided to return and finish the job he had started hours earlier?

Or were there demons in this strange uncharted land?

He could feel his heart pounding inside his chest as trepidation filled every pore of his body. The sound grew louder and the mist began to move hypnotically before his eyes as he strained to see who or what was approaching.

Only one thing was certain. He was scared stiff.

Denying every instinct he possessed, Slim took one step forward and lowered his hand to his side. His fingertips touched the grip of his gun but he left it firmly secured in its aged holster.

'Who are you?' he called out through the vaporous fog that froze his skin as it lapped over him like an invisible tidal wave.

Then Walker saw the impenetrable mist directly before his face swirl violently. Something had been thrown through it.

Before he could move a muscle, the six-foot-long lance landed between his cowboy boots. Slim looked down at it and focused on the two feathers that were tied just behind the long metal spearhead. He recognized the distinctive markings on the wooden shaft of the weapon.

Suddenly he had the answer he sought.

'Apache!' he muttered under his breath.

EIGHT

Since time itself began, this land had been a place where few Indian tribes ventured willingly. The bleached bones of those who underestimated the fury of this land were littered across its scarlet sand.

The valleys between the towering mesas held no taboos; the land was not sacred in any known way to any of the nomadic tribes, but had become notorious as being a place where death stalked even the well equipped.

It had a thousand ways of killing unsuspecting intruders. Like a demonic entity, it used each and every one of them whenever an opportunity arose to do so. Few creatures could live for long within its boundaries and most did not have the courage to even try.

But there was one exception.

The rugged Apache knew every square inch of this strange landscape. It held no fear for them because they had been forced into far worse places since the Spanish and white settlers had driven them from their ancestral homelands.

Defiantly, they still survived where others had not.

It was said that the Apache could live on fresh air and the tears of the Great Spirit.

No hardship could break this unique people. They were made of tougher stuff than most of humanity. The Apache people refused to simply disappear and fade into the historical records as had been the fate of so many of their fellow Indians.

They had to be tough because for centuries fate had dealt them one cruel hand after another.

The dozen mounted warriors eased their painted ponies closer to the startled man and studied him closely. For some strange reason they had been watching Slim Walker since he had first entered the wide valley of mesas in pursuit of his evil and deadly sibling. Yet the twins, like every other rider who had entered this lethal place, had not seen the eyes of the Apache watching and following them. The warriors could somehow blend into the very landscape itself.

Only being seen when they wanted to be.

Curiosity had brought the dishevelled riders out from their hiding-places when they had noticed the courage of the man who had been left for dead by the rider on the black stallion. A rider whom they recognized by his distinctive mount.

The Apache honoured courage above nearly all things and they recognized it in Slim Walker. They wondered why had he not used the gun he wore on his hip to defend himself or to try and kill the man who had attempted to kill him. To the warriors who had been watching, this seemed odd.

Yet they knew that there had to be some reason why one man would not return fire on another who had ambushed him and then tried to take his life.

Then the riders on their thin painted ponies wondered why he had continued to follow, rather than take the safer option and return the way he had come.

To the hardened Apache braves, this made Slim Walker worth investigating.

Slim managed to remain upright and stare helplessly at the twelve horsemen who faced him. They had thick blankets wrapped around their shoulders and a few wore hats decorated with eagle-feathers. Unlike Walker, they were prepared for the dramatic climatic change.

He noticed the horses lowering their heads and snatching at the sparse sagebrush whenever their masters allowed the crude reins to slacken.

Slim Walker knew that these warriors were capable of killing him faster than it took to blink an eye, but they had not done so and that gave him heart. Unlike his brother, these men were not mindless killers.

The oldest-looking of the riders had grey hair cut abruptly just below his earlobes. His eyes were hooded and showed little emotion as he teased his pony around the silent man. They were inspecting him as if their paths had previously crossed.

A cold shiver ran up Walker's spine. What if these men had encountered Zane in the past? Would they make him pay for something he had no knowledge of? Slim had lost count of the times when he had been mistaken for his heartless brother.

The horses continued to circle him.

Just watching the riders moving around him astride the backs of their mounts, made him feel giddy. Walker felt his legs weaken again and tried to remain upright as the curious riders continued to move their ponies around him. But he had gone too long without water and suddenly fell to the ground.

With every last ounce of what was left of

his willpower, he forced his eyes to remain open as he lay beside the long feathered lance.

The Apache with the grey hair said something.

Walker watched helplessly as the ponies stopped. Then he saw two of the Apache braves dismounting and moving towards him.

One of them knelt down beside him on the sand. He felt the hand on his temple. Suddenly Slim's fevered mind began to play tricks on him.

Everything in his line of vision started to spin until there was nothing left but blackness.

NINE

The outlaw sat perched outside the massive cave high in the canyon wall staring down at the land which was as merciless as himself. For roughly two years this had been a safe haven for Zane Walker. Its sheer remoteness from civilization made it an ideal hideout from where he could plan and execute his brutal bank raids. He inhaled deeply on the cigarette that he had just lit and thought about the sight of his brother falling from his mount back in the wide valley. As the smoke drifted through his teeth, he laughed. He knew that by killing the horse, he had more than certainly done for the master. Yet there was no guilt in his mind.

He was incapable of feeling that emotion. You had to have a conscience to do so. He had none.

Zane Walker had not one ounce of humanity flowing through his rancid veins. He had reached a depth of depravity that few could even imagine existed. The ruthless outlaw had grown worse as each

70

passing day led into another. At first he had been satisfied by just fighting with his fists, then he had progressed to using the jagged ends of broken bottles to secure his dubious victories. Then knives had made mere beatings turn into brutal killings. Yet even that failed to satisfy Zane Walker's insatiable appetite, for he had tasted blood. Guns and pistols had found his willing nature a breeding-ground for total destruction.

At the age of fifteen, when most people were still satisfied with enjoying the last embers of their childhood, he had already started carving notches on to the wooden handles of his gun grips.

They say that killing can become a habit that some find impossible to give up. Zane Walker had become such a creature and could or would not stop his evil ways.

There was a power in being able to destroy people without a second thought. He had that power and used it whenever the mood took him.

Year after year his atrocities had gone unchecked for there seemed to be no one capable of stopping his relentless journey into the bowels of hell. Those who had tried had ended up as just another notch on his guns.

There seemed to be no sane reason for his being the way he was and perhaps that was the answer. For insanity often hides itself inside the handsomest of guises. Zane Walker was, like his brother, handsome. Yet there was not a single spark of humanity within him.

There never had been.

Some had said that it was mere jealousy caused because Zane looked like Slim. It had soured him. But others who had been closer knew the cruel truth.

Zane had always been totally envious of his twin brother because Slim had been a hard worker who could create things with his bare hands. People praised the elder Walker twin and that created a hatred and envy that had grown like a cancer in the mind of the less stable brother. Some had said Zane showed all the signs of being insane, but as he was the spitting image of his twin, it was hard to accept.

Zane had always been of a dark ruthless disposition, the total opposite of the good natured Slim. The child who pulled the wings from butterflies had progressed to killing anyone who even looked at him in a way that displeased him. The outlaw refused to walk in the shadow of his slightly older identical brother and had vowed to make everyone sit up and take notice of his existence.

Only his existence.

He had wanted to kill Slim since they were small. It had been his first and only remaining thought that he had brought into adulthood.

The outlaw flicked the ash off the cigarette, screwed his eyes up and studied Skull Canyon. Even bathed in moonlight, it was an awesome sight. A place that lingered in a man's memory until it had found the part of the brain that nurtured nightmares.

It had been an accident that he had found the place that so many others feared. Deep in the very heart of the deadly valley of mesas, Zane had discovered Skull Canyon.

It had been two years earlier, when Zane Walker had been fleeing a posse of rope-swingers that the ruthless outlaw found himself riding into a land that even hardened lawmen refused to enter.

Thrashing his black stallion with his long reins he had ridden hard across the red sand and not even noticed that his pursuers had ceased following him hours earlier. Even though he was low on water and his saddlebags were weighed down by the proceeds of a blood-chilling bank robbery, he carried on.

Walker had not noticed the temperature rising with every stride that his mount was taking. Faster and faster he had travelled with no thought for himself or his faithful steed's welfare. All he could think about was reaching the other side of the unholy terrain he had accidentally ridden into.

A sane man would have quit and tried to make his way back out of the deadly land whilst there was still time. But the outlaw was far from sane and drove on.

Walker did not have the same fears as normal men. He thought himself invulnerable; he forced the black horse to continue galloping across the flat landscape even though it was exhausted and ready to drop. The powerful stallion continued galloping because it feared its master more than death itself.

The cruel rider whipped his horse into the blinding heat haze until something directly ahead of him blocked his progress. That had been when Walker had encountered the hunting party of Apache braves seeking anything edible to kill that might fill the bellies of their families.

Hauling his reins in to his chest, Zane Walker had sat watching the startled Indians through the dust that had been kicked up from his stallion's hoofs.

It had not taken him long to work out that they, unlike himself, were not heavily armed. His cold calculating eyes had spotted the single-shot rifles hanging from the necks of their painted ponies next to the swollen water-pouches. He knew that those rifles were no match for his fourteen-shot Winchester repeating rifle.

Suddenly the expression of the horseman had altered. There were people to kill and he felt in the mood to oblige.

The Apache braves had started to ride wide of the stranger within their midst when Walker had swiftly pulled his faithful repeating rifle out from its saddle scabbard, cocked it and started firing.

He had plucked three of them off the backs of their mounts before their blood had reached the sand. The remaining horrified Indians used the cover of the cloud of gunsmoke that hung on the hot afternoon air as their opportunity to ride off into the maze of high twisting rocky towers before Walker had time to train his sights on them as well.

Outraged by the sight of the dust coming off the unshod pony-hoofs, Zane Walker had ridden up to the fallen Apaches and ensured that they were dead by blasting each of them once more where they lay.

He rounded up the three ponies and removed the large water-pouches that were hung over the necks of the animals. After securing them to his own saddle, he swung the stallion around and then began to laugh at the dust left by the fleeing Indian warriors.

Spurring his mount, Zane set off in hot pursuit of the remaining riders. He wanted them dead as well. Yet no matter how hard he drove his razor-sharp spurs into the flesh of his faithful black steed, he could not catch the terrified Apaches.

His lathered-up horse was weighed down by the weight of the precious water and the silver coins in his saddle-bags.

Yet he refused to quit his pursuit until, to his utter surprise, he rode into a dead-end canyon and found that he had discovered a place that lay deep in the heart of the maze of rocky peaks, where water flowed from high above. A place that, for some unknown reason, was littered with countless human skulls.

Zane Walker sat beneath the rocky overhang

high above the ground and tossed the butt of his smoke down into the place that he had named Skull Canyon.

Numerous caves were filled with more than a thousand human skulls. Whose skulls they were and why they were here, he could only imagine.

Walker had found a natural refuge in one of the most deadly places on the face of the earth. The natural spring came from high above and ran down the side of the rockface next to the high cave that he had used since that first time he had discovered the hidden canyon. The water was clean and collected in a pool below, where he stabled his black stallion.

No one else knew of this canyon.

This was where he brought all his ill-gotten gains.

It belonged to him.

This was his Skull Canyon.

TEN

Sheriff Marvin Peabody was one of those rare men who looked part of the horse he was riding. He fitted its saddle and just became part of the creature as it moved over the soft sand towards the rim of the cliff edge. His deputy was another of those men who rode well but seemed to walk with an exaggerated gait.

The large moon had climbed high into the dark-blue sky since the two riders had set out from Broken Gulch. It had taken them two hours just to reach the edge of the terrifying drop. But neither man was in a hurry. They knew when it was wise to be cautious.

The sheriff stopped his grey horse and spat.

Peabody lifted his binoculars off the horn of his saddle, put them to his eyes and studied the vastness below their high vantage point. If Zane Walker was down there, he thought, he was well hidden. The sheriff moved the glasses slowly to his right until he had taken in the entire panorama. He could make out small trails of smoke rising from two separate spots amid the rocky towers, but that meant nothing. He knew that there were Apaches down there someplace. They preferred the deadly valleys to the company of whites. Peabody knew why.

The mule had not given Tom Smith any trouble since they had set out and that was something both men were grateful for. This was not a terrain that favoured temperamental pack-animals. Smith did not want the cantankerous animal falling off the high cliff and pulling him over with it.

'You see anythin', Sheriff?'

'Yep.'

'What?'

'A lotta rocks, boy.' Sheriff Peabody hung the binoculars back on the saddle horn and sighed heavily before spitting again.

'Where do ya figure Walker is?' Smith asked. He unscrewed the stopper of his canteen and took a long drink of the cold water.

'Hard to say, Tom. But I got me a few ideas.' Peabody toyed with his reins gently and stared down into the moonlit landscape. It was a maze of canyons which led to a wide valley. Mesas rose from far below them for as far as the eye could see. The sheriff rubbed his whiskers and waited for his companion to draw level with him.

'How long do you figure it'll take us to get down there, Sheriff?' Smith asked as he stood in his stirrups to get an even better view of the deadly land below them.

Peabody sighed and spat out a gob of dark spittle. Both men watched it fall into the depths.

'I reckon we'll be down there before noon.'

Smith pulled out his pocket-watch, snapped open its lid and turned its glass so that the moonlight illuminated its face.

'That's fifteen hours. You say it'll take us fifteen hours to get down there?'

'Yep. There is a quicker way down, but that calls for us to leap off this cliff.' The sheriff smiled and then tapped his spurs into the sides of his grey. The wily lawman started along the rim towards the crude natural trail that he had used a dozen times before.

'What if he ain't down there at all, Sheriff?' The deputy snapped the lid of his watch shut before sliding it into his deep jacket-pocket. He pulled the rope that was tied to the bridle of the mule and then urged his horse on. He followed the older rider carefully.

Peabody looked over his shoulder.

'Then we'll have us a picnic, boy.'

The younger rider kept his horse following directly behind the tail of the grey mount.

ELEVEN

It was a dark place that Slim Walker had fallen into when he had eventually lost his battle with exhaustion and thirst. There was only so far a man could push his body before it shattered into a thousand pieces, somehow he had exceeded that point valiantly.

Wherever his tortured mind had retreated to, it was an unholy place like the desert he had fought so doggedly. Explosions came from all around him as he continued his reluctant descent into the mysterious abyss. Flames leapt out from all around him as he desperately tried to fight his way back to the real world from wherever it was that had claimed him. A thousand deafening drums seemed to beat inside the black clouds which filled Slim Walker's nightmare as if daring to compete with the massive blasts.

A symphony of wailing children's cries echoed all about him and chilled his blood. Slim searched and searched but could not find out where they were coming from.

Then he saw flaming arrows coming straight at him. Slim tried to beat them off with his bare hands. But one by one the arrowheads tore into him.

Yet there was no pain with these deadly arrows.

Suddenly he noticed the Apache warriors mounted all around him aiming their bows at him. They fired again and he saw another volley of fire arrows cutting through the darkness. Turning he saw the blazing sun blocking the way out of this place. He was trapped.

Slim thrashed out and then tried to run away from the Apaches but his feet began to sink.

Quicksand!

The more he struggled, the faster he watched his body disappearing into the soft sand. As he clawed at the ground all about him he felt himself being sucked down by some strange power beneath its surface.

A million snapping skulls replaced the faces of the warriors and began to move closer to his helpless body. He tried to scream for help but the sand filled his mouth and he felt himself being pulled down.

Slim was being dragged down into the very ground itself as if claws had sunk into the flesh of his legs. He fought like a tiger and tried to reach the surface again but they had the better of him and were pulling him down into the jaws of Satan.

He seemed to be able to see the horned demon laughing at him yet he knew that this was impossible. This was not real, he told himself repeatedly. This was just a bad dream.

Once more he opened his mouth but nothing came out. The skulls followed him as he fell into another massive cave. Flames leapt from out of the ground at the bottom of the strange place.

Slim floated on the licking flames as skulls came at him from all sides. Their teeth tore at him, but he felt no pain.

Again he fought with his fists but could not seem to make any impact on the demented creatures. They bit at his knuckles until he could actually see the blood pouring from his torn and ripped flesh. Now he could feel the pain. Every sinew in his body seemed to hurt as he continued being devoured by the monstrous balls of fire.

Suddenly he felt cold as if ice had been thrown over his burning body, but there was no ice. The torturous flames were like freezing cubes of ice.

He continued to fall as once more the sound of explosions deafened him. Then he saw a mirror rising from beneath him out of the smoke. It was a massive mirror covered in blood. Higher and higher it ascended. When it was level with him he was able to see the image laughing at him.

What madman was this, he thought.

He tried to lash out with his fists but his arms could no longer move. The laughter became deafening.

Slim screwed up his eyes as more freezing flames burned every stitch of clothing from his bruised and battered body. The laughter was now insane and then he recognized the face in the mirror.

It was his own face.

Yet the eyes were hollow and the head rocked back and forth as it continued laughing at him. Then he saw the horns on its forehead.

This was not his own image, he thought. Yet it looked like him. It was Zane!

Slim tried to turn away from the reflection but it chased his every move, always remaining right in front of his face allowing him to see nothing but the crazed face mocking him.

Then a rifle barrel protruded from the

mirror and aimed straight at him. He tried to flee, but it was impossible to get away from the cold rifle barrel. A deafening blast came from the rifle and Slim felt the bullet hitting him in his heart.

He tried to cry out but his voice had deserted him.

The face in the mirror grew larger and larger as it hovered directly over his helpless body. Everything around him started to shake as if an earthquake had just struck this nightmarish place. Slim looked up at the insane face laughing hysterically down at him. Then the bloodstained glass shattered into a million fragments and fell like minute daggers.

As the glass showered over him he expected it to skewer him into the ground. Yet it did not.

As he lay waiting for yet more pain to strike his helpless body, water, not glass flowed over his face and body. He felt himself awaking and yet was still terrified that reality might just be worse than the haunting nightmare he had finally escaped from.

For a few seemingly endless moments, he kept his eyes shut tight and tried to gather his wits. The utter relief of his knowing that finally he was back in the land of the living gave him courage. His mind raced as he tried to assemble the events of the hours before his collapse together in one bundle. It was no easy task.

Slim could feel the soothing hands bathing his face, neck and torso with cold water. He was being gently brought back from the brink of death and was grateful. He could hear the crackling of dried wood spitting from a large camp-fire nearby to his left. Muffled voices spoke in a tongue that he could not understand as children sobbed from a dozen or more yards away. Slim knew that the sobbing was not caused by any infliction of punishment, but by hunger.

Slim Walker blinked hard and then saw the faces of the Apache braves all around him. There were others here as well. Females and children all gathered around a roaring camp-fire. Every eye was on him as he lay on a coarse blanket on the hard ground.

Walker raised himself up on one elbow and noticed that they were on a ledge just inside the entrance of a large cave. He touched his face and felt the water running over his tender burned skin. An ear-splitting thunderclap shook the entire mountain range yet none of the Apaches moved a muscle. They just continued watching him with curious, sad eyes.

An elderly woman was kneeling next to him. It had been she who had been bathing the fever from his nightmares, he thought. He smiled.

She nodded at Walker and offered him a ladle of water.

He accepted and drank the ice-cold liquid.

'Thanks, ma'am,' he said.

The Apache with the grey hair stepped closer and then sat down next to the right shoulder of the weak man. His face seemed puzzled.

'You saved my life. Thanks.' Slim sighed.

'Your dreams were filled with monsters,' the warrior said bluntly.

Slim breathed out heavily. 'Yep. I saw me some monsters.'

The Apache touched Walker's face.

'You have same face as an evil man who hides far off in one of the canyons. We have tried to find him but he kills my young braves so they cannot reveal his hiding-place.'

'So he's down there?'

'Yes, but there are so many canyons and valleys.' The Apache shook his head before staring hard at Walker's face again. 'I do not understand. How can two men have same face?'

'He's my brother,' came the simple reply.

'He bad. He kill many of my people.' The Apache snorted. 'We not harm him but he kill my braves. Why?'

'He's just bad. Real bad.' Slim sighed heavily.

The old warrior stared out at the moonlit land below them. He was thoughtful.

'He your brother and he try to kill you. This man is not like other men. He should die but we are not skilled in the ways of killing men.'

Slim rolled on to his side and looked hard at the impassive face of his benefactor.

'I reckon that's why I've been chasing him, my friend. I've been thinking that I have to kill him.'

The warrior nodded. 'This is right.'

'When I was asleep I heard many things and now that I'm awake I can see what filled my mind with so many thoughts. But there was one thing that I still can't figure out.' Slim paused and rubbed his face.

'What did you see that worries you?' the Indian asked.

'I saw hundreds of skulls.'

The Apache turned his head and looked

straight at Slim Walker.

'You have dreamt of the valley of skulls? But how?'

Slim sat up and rested his hand on the warrior's shoulder. He knew that once again he had seen through his brother's evil eyes.

'You mean that there's a valley filled with skulls?'

The Apache pointed at the mountainous peaks to the east.

'Yes, my friend. It is over there, but we do not go to that place.'

'That could be where my brother is hiding out.' Slim Walker suddenly felt his strength and determination returning. 'If it is, that's where I have to go.'

'We will help you. We will take you to this place.'

Slim Walker stared at the moon directly above them until black clouds obscured it from view. Thunder rumbled noisy as bolts of lightning splintered through the cold air. He rose to his feet.

TWELVE

Rain fell violently across the valley of towering mesas, yet it was dry around the Apache encampment on the high ridge. Slim Walker watched in awe as the far-off thunder and lightning grew worse. That was where the grey-haired Apache elder had said the valley of skulls lay. It troubled him.

Would the storm help or hinder him?

As he was led down the steep stone steps, carved out by countless generations of Apache, he stared through the moonlight at the rain falling over their destination. Only yesterday he had prayed for even one drop of the precious liquid, yet now he felt that it might be his undoing.

What was this strange place that the Indians called the valley of skulls? He had tried to block the question from his mind, but a mixture of confusion and fear continued nagging at him. The only thing that made any sense in his weary mind was that he knew this would be exactly the sort of hideout Zane would choose for himself.

The macabre had always suited his evil brother. Zane Walker would have relished the idea of being surrounded by the brutal reminders of his own deadly profession. Slim wondered why anyone would store so many skulls in a deserted canyon in the first place. Then his mind drifted to who the victims and victors might have been.

The Apache with the grey hair had said that the skulls had been there since time began. That chilled Slim Walker's bones. By the Indian's description of the place it sounded more like a dead-end canyon and not a valley, but he was not about to argue with any of his companions.

Slim knew that he owed them his life and wondered whether he might ever be able to replay that priceless debt.

But first he had to survive.

Exactly how he might achieve that when faced by his ruthless brother, was something Slim chose not to dwell upon. He paced after the three shorter Indians with a blanket wrapped around his shoulders towards the small gulch where they kept their mounts.

Walker watched the young braves as they expertly cut out four of the small horses from the herd.

He leaned against the rockface and gazed through the eerie moonlight, which somehow still managed to illuminate this part of the vast land, at the storm clouds that were directly above the place the Apaches called the valley of skulls. Rain was driving down over the entire area, yet he and his companions were bone-dry.

The angry storm was getting more and more violent with every passing heartbeat. It was also spreading out in all directions. The constant sound of deafening thunder rumbled through the valleys and flashes of lightning temporarily blinded him.

The sky was being lit up like a Fourth of July fireworks party as the storm got progressively more ferocious. Electrical light rippled from one horizon to the next making the prairie appear even more unforgiving.

The storm was engulfing the entire sky. It was becoming a monster bent on the total destruction of anything beneath its lethal canopy.

Slim saw the young braves handing him a crude rope which was tied around the bottom jaw of a small pinto pony and looped in such a fashion behind its ears that it served very effectively as reins. He accepted the rope and looked at the horse carefully.

He had never ridden an Indian pony before and silently wondered what differences there might be in the training of such animals. Walker had heard that the Apache riders had their own secret signals to control a pony which were quite opposite to those generally used by whites.

After ensuring that the horse blanket was tied on to the back of the skittish pony, Walker wrapped the rope around his wrist several times, then grabbed the white mane tightly in his left hand. Somehow he managed to pull his tall, lean frame over the back of the pony, then he sat upright behind the shoulders of the stocky animal.

He had never been nervous when it came to riding until now. His feet searched for stirrups but then he realized that there weren't any. The thought of trying to balance without stirrups or a saddle horn were daunting, but he knew that beggars could not be choosers.

Slim steadied himself carefully and noticed the smiling faces of the three Apaches as they swung themselves on to their mounts quickly and easily. They were amused.

The four riders sat for a few moments and Walker wondered what they were waiting for. Then he heard the moccasins of the grey-haired Apache elder coming down the stone steps carrying Slim's gunbelt. The Indian handed the gunbelt to Slim, then entered the crude corral and led out his own pony. He held on to the mane and threw himself on to its back.

'You ready to go find evil brother, my friend?' the Apache asked as he drew his pony level with the others.

Slim pushed the brim of his Stetson back off his brow and looked hard at the wise face.

'I ought to know your name and you mine, *amigo*.'

'I called Heronis,' the grey-haired man informed him. 'I am Chief of my people.'

'They call me Slim,' Walker said. He wondered how many of these people might have once roamed this land. He had counted fewer than forty up in the cave. It saddened him.

The Indian nodded. 'Good name. You follow us. We take you to valley of skulls.'

Walker nervously held the rope reins in his hand, gripped the ribs of the pony firmly with his legs and somehow succeeded in making his pony follow the four others. Within a hundred yards he had drawn level with them but knew that that was because they had slowed to an almost halt, waiting for him to master riding the strange pony.

The five riders made their way through the maze of moonlit canyons at a slow deliberate pace.

The night was still young and the storm was still raging over the far-off Skull Canyon. None of them wished to reach their destination too quickly, for different reasons. Slim knew that once he reached Skull Canyon he would have to face Zane and fight. There was only one way to fight a man like his brother and that was to the death.

The four Apaches knew that they were riding to confront a man who had already killed many of their brothers in cold blood. He was not a man they wished to encounter face on. Zane had too many lethal weapons in his arsenal, and was deadly with all of them.

The closer they got, the more they could feel the power of the storm all around them. Rain began to touch them as they rode on and on but none of them seemed to notice.

Slim Walker was only too aware that the next few hours might prove to be his last.

THIRTEEN

The narrow trail leading down to the valley of mesas was not an easy one to negotiate at the best of times. In daylight it was merely dangerous, at night it was utterly treacherous but once wet, whether during the hours of daylight or darkness, it became simply deadly.

What had been a dusty bone-hard trail was now little more than a steep and muddy death-trap. Sheriff Marvin Peabody and his deputy Tom Smith had been caught out by the sudden arrival of storm clouds that had swept in over the eastern edge of the vast rocky region.

They were only an eighth of the way down the difficult trail when the sky above them had suddenly gone dark and then exploded into something neither men had experienced before. The moody clouds had rumbled angrily above them and completely obliterated the bright moon which the lawmen had been using to light their way down the twisting trail that hugged the rocks.

With no light to guide them, both men were suddenly riding blindly down a route that they could only guess at. Then when they thought it could get no worse, it did.

The deafening thunderclaps above them mixed with the frightening lightning flashes made controlling their horses and pack-mule almost impossible.

Then the rain had started to fall, slowly at first, then with more and more ferocity.

Very quickly the trail beneath the hoofs of their horses became treacherous. The two lawmen remained in their saddles knowing that all they could do was to hang on to their reins and try to guide their frightened mounts through the darkness.

Soon, every other option had disappeared.

The sheriff considered hauling his reins in and stopping his mount but knew that with Tom so close behind him, that would have caused total confusion. It was impossible to try and turn their horses around on the narrow trail as muddy rainwater swept off the rockface and flowed over the surface of the trail.

Somehow they had to try and keep their animals moving whilst they prayed to be delivered from this insanity.

Peabody was anxious enough about controlling his grey but knew that his deputy had an even harder job. Tom Smith not only had to keep his horse from panicking but also keep the pack-mule under control.

Any one of the three animals could bring the others off the high mountain trail and cause them to fall to their doom.

Every few feet the sheriff would turn and look back but he could see nothing through the driving continuous rain. Only when the lightning flashed was there any light and then it took every ounce of his strength and skill just to keep his own grey mount from spooking and galloping off into the deadly abyss beside him.

The wily older lawman had considered dismounting and trying to lead his horse on foot but knew that there was no way he could control a terrified horse whilst standing on the ground. His and Smith's only hope was to remain in their saddles, however scary it might continue to get.

A bolt of lightning forked down from above them and caused part of the rockface behind them to explode sending boulders falling into the darkness. Only a few seconds later the deafening sound of thunder had resounded in their ears. Peabody gritted his teeth and clung to his reins for all he was worth, fighting with the animal to prevent it from running forward into the unknown.

Tom Smith's horse reared up and was only controlled by the younger man's strength. The mule began to wail in distress behind them, but again was stopped from bolting by the skilful deputy.

Neither man had uttered a word since the storm had overtaken them. They had to concentrate totally on their seemingly endless journey.

They were committed to continuing down the trail like a pair of blind horsemen and were tormented by the knowledge that they were helpless to do anything about it.

Then another jagged fork of lightning came twisting out of the black clouds above them. This time its white-hot tip hit the rocks a mere few yards above the head of the struggling sheriff.

It sounded like a dozen cannons being fired at exactly the same moment. Both riders reeled in their saddles at the sheer force and noise of the massive explosion.

Boulders of a thousand differing sizes and shapes blasted off the wall of a rock and showered down over Peabody and his faithful grey.

Smith reined in and watched in horror as

sheet lightning above them lit up the horrific scene in all its gory detail.

Rocks came down amid the rain all around the older horseman as the sheriff fought to keep his mount in check. But one of the boulders was too big and too accurate.

The startled deputy screamed out in horror as he saw Peabody being hit off his saddle by the large rock. For a moment Tom was about to leap from his own horse and try to reach his friend but as another flash lit up the angry sky, he knew it was too late.

He had just caught a fleeting glimpse of the sheriff disappearing over the side of the muddy edge of the trail whilst the grey horse galloped off down the steep route.

Tom Smith drew his horse level with the spot slowly and stared down into the blackness below him. Mud was flowing over the lip of the trail road like a continuous waterfall. Reluctantly he urged his horse to continue.

Peabody was gone.

FOURTEEN

Dawn had come early across the strange landscape but there was no let-up in the ferocity of the storm. Like an angry God trying to punish anyone or anything below it, it continued to unleash its venom. Earth-shaking explosions of thunder and fiery bolts of lightning had not ceased for more than a few minutes during the previous six hours.

The sun somehow managed to filter into the maze of countless canyons after stretching out across the wide valley, but its warmth did nothing to stop the storm. It showed no sign of stopping at any time in the near or distant future.

The continuous rain had turned the red sand into a muddy quagmire yet this had not deterred Slim Walker and his four Apache companions from their mission. They rode steadily on and on towards their goal. Nothing could stop them on their quest to find the vicious outlaw.

The five horsemen had managed to make

good progress despite everything that nature had thrown at them. Winding their way through the twisting canyons for hour after hour, they eventually slowed their pace as the Apache chief raised his hand. Heronis stopped his pony and was quickly followed by his three warriors and Walker.

The hooded eyes of the warrior stared up into the high rocks as rain pounded down from the black clouds. Even when the sky lit up with flashes of lightning, Heronis did not blink or flinch. He was searching for the man they feared in case he lay in wait for them. Only when satisfied that Zane Walker was nowhere to be seen did he lower his hand and turn to face his companions.

Slim moved his mount to the side of the thoughtful Indian.

'What's wrong, Heronis?'

'This place you seek, Slim,' the chief replied, pointing through the driving rain at the wet rocks that faced them.

Slim Walker could see nothing except yet another shining wall of solid granite. He was confused.

'Where? I don't see no skulls, Heronis.'

The grey-haired Apache slid off the back of his bedraggled pony and waited until Slim had copied his actions. The two men left the three other braves and made their way through the six-inch-deep mud toward the wet rockface. With water pouring constantly down its surface, it seemed almost like a gigantic mirror.

The tall cowboy screwed up his eyes and then saw what his friend was pointing at. The opening to the canyon they sought was almost impossible to see at first. Nature had disguised it well for some purpose.

'Now you see?' Heronis asked.

'Yep.' Slim nodded.

Slim stopped and adjusted the heavy blanket that had kept the cold night air off his shoulders and back for so many hours. It was now soaking wet and three times its original weight, but it had served one purpose.

It had kept the pistol in its holster dry.

Heronis moved cautiously now. He feared the evil twin brother of his companion more than any other man that he had ever encountered. The Apache moved to the high rocky wall and stared into the opening of Skull Canyon.

Slim edged his way to the man's side and yet they could see nothing from where they were standing. The route into the canyon twisted several times before the true magnitude of the hidden canyon became evident.

'I reckon this is where we part company, *amigo*.' Walker smiled and began to head through the corridor of rocks. He felt a firm hand grip his arm and stopped. The cowboy turned and looked straight into the face of the Indian. 'What's the matter?'

'I go with you,' Heronis said, releasing Slim's arm. He gripped the handle of the long knife tucked into his sodden belt.

Slim shook his head.

'This ain't your fight, Chief. Zane is my brother and my responsibility. I go alone.'

'Evil brother kill you easy,' Heronis said bluntly. 'He already killed many of my people and he will try to kill you. You not get him on your own. We go together.'

There was an insistence in the voice of the Apache chieftain that made Slim listen.

'Are you sure?'

Heronis nodded. 'Me sure, Slim.'

'Thanks, *amigo*.' Slim felt an invisible weight being lifted off his broad shoulders. 'I reckon that I ain't gonna last long on my own. Zane is too good a shot.'

The Apache looked hard into the face of the young man.

'You not die this day, Slim.'

'I sure hope that you're right.'

'Heronis is right.' There was a strange confidence in the words of the elderly Apache warrior. Slim noted that he gave no such assurances for himself or his fellow braves.

Heronis turned and signalled to his three braves. They each dropped from the backs of their mounts and walked slowly through the muddy water to the sides of the two men. They carried their small bows and quivers full of arrows.

Heronis spoke to his young followers and they all nodded as if agreeing to some master plan that their chief had ordered them to obey. The braves moved away from Heronis and Slim and began to make their way into the mouth of Skull Canyon.

Slim pulled the blanket from his shoulders and dropped it next to the pile of other discarded blankets. He swallowed hard and took a deep breath.

He moved silently forward with the chief.

Slim wondered if it would be possible to get close to his brother without Zane's honed killer-instincts becoming aware of their presence. He also wondered how he could actually defeat the twin who had always managed to beat him at everything.

For some say that you have to have a 'killer

instinct' to beat your opponents. Some have it in abundance whilst others do not have a single trace of it in their entire bodies.

Slim knew that, for the first time in their lives, he and Zane would have to do battle.

It would be a battle to the death because that was the only way that his identical sibling fought. Even now, Slim found it hard even to feel any anger, but knew that he had to try.

To fail would be no better than committing suicide.

Zane had not an ounce of mercy in him. He would take pleasure in destroying the man who had his own image branded on his handsome face.

Slim knew that given half a chance his brother would also kill Heronis and the three young braves too. He could not allow that to happen to such a proud race of people. There were far too few of them left as it was.

The cowboy flicked the safety loop off his pistol, drew the weapon from its holster and cocked its hammer carefully. He then checked his gunbelt strapped to his narrow hips, pulled six of the bullets from it and pushed them into the back pocket of his soaked denim pants. He doubted if he would have much time to reload the weapon, but knew it would be far easier to find the bullets in his pants pocket than fumbling for them in his gunbelt.

'Come on, boys. Let's take us a look,' he said, leading the four Apaches through the torrential downpour into the mouth of Skull Canyon.

The wildest of animals often know when they are in danger. So it was with Zane Walker. He had slept high in his cave for more than seven hours totally untroubled by the raging storm. Yet even through the deafening sound of the rain that hammered down with unyielding persistence, he awoke suddenly when the five figures entered the canyon.

He lay on his back beneath his blankets in the dry cave and stared at the dancing lights in the cave wall caused by the rising sun penetrating the curtain of rainwater flowing over the mouth of the cave entrance.

Without even knowing why, the fingers of Zane's left hand plucked the Colt .45 from his holster.

Somehow, he knew that his brother was not dead after all.

His thumb pulled back the hammer until it fully locked.

FIFTEEN

Marvin Peabody lay in a sea of mud at the foot of the massive mountain. It was obvious that the deep soft mud had saved his life but he could not remember anything about it. He knew that if he had not been knocked unconscious he would have probably died of fright during the fall. Rain still beat down on to the land around him as Peabody slowly found himself regaining his senses. The sheriff blinked hard and then realized that his lower half was submerged in the sticky soft mud.

The sheriff knew that although this mud had probably saved his life when he had landed into it, there was a real good chance that if he made a false move, it might suck him under. For several minutes the lawman used every ounce of his strength just to move his legs in a bid to find something solid enough for him to stand on. The brown goo was starting to set now that the morning sun was warming up the valley and canyons. Peabody began to fear being trapped here once the rain stopped and the mud set into a slab of baked adobe.

He used the tentative footing to stabilize himself and looked around the area for a way out of his predicament. He spotted a few boulders piled up where they had fallen next to the edge of the massive mud-hole. To reach them, he had to take the biggest gamble of his life and try to propel his body up and over the clinging mud. He took a deep gulp of breath and carefully bent his knees. He was scared as his chest began to sink that he would not have the power to force himself back out of the brown slime.

Peabody forced himself up and reached out with his arms. He felt his boots losing contact with the solid ground beneath the mud. He managed to force his body out of the mud except for his legs from the knees down.

The sheriff landed in a belly flop on to the surface of the unstable surface. For a moment he did not move a muscle. He just lay on the strange texture of the mud and wondered what he could or should do next. Raising his head a few inches he could see that the rocks he sought were a mere four or five feet away from his fingertips. Peabody knew that he had to reach those rocks in order to drag himself on to solid ground.

The lawman felt his outstretched body slowly sinking into the mud. He knew that he had to act and act now.

Somehow Peabody's fingers managed to claw at the mud and pull his lean body towards the rocks. Inch by precious inch he advanced towards them. With every breath he felt his body sinking beneath the surface of the strange mud, but he carried on. Peabody raised his right leg until his boot reappeared from the mud, then he eased himself forward again. Then his other boot managed to escape the suction of the mud. Finding his whole body now on the surface, the sheriff crawled for all he was worth until he felt solid ground beneath his fingertips.

Peabody rolled over on to his back and opened his mouth to drink the rain which continued to fall. He needed every drop of its precious life-giving gift to renew his exhausted body.

His mind searched for answers.

Where was he?

How had he got here?

For what seemed like an eternity, the lawman could remember nothing.

Everything was a mass of confusion.

His eyes tried to search the landscape for

answers but there was none. He managed to roll over and to get up on his knees but then fell on to his back again. He hurt like hell. Every sinew and bone felt as if it had been kicked by a mule.

The rain pounded like devilish torture on to his face. He somehow found enough strength to haul himself upright until he was sitting. He stared through his bushy eyebrows as water dripped off them. For a few fleeting moments, he wondered where his old Stetson might be, then he shuddered.

The rumble of angry thunder vibrated off the rocks which surrounded him and made the sheriff jolt in terror. His mind suddenly began to awaken from the nightmare that had in fact, been a reality.

As he looked up, he suddenly knew that it had all been real.

Every one of the terrifying images that had filled his weary mind had actually happened.

Sheriff Peabody knew that he had been riding up on the steep trail far above this place. He remembered the lightning and how he had been knocked off his startled grey mount and thrown out into the darkness.

Peabody looked up at the high rocks and gulped.

Had he fallen all that way?

The lawman clawed his way back to his feet and leaned heavily on the mountain wall. Mud still flowed down its surface from far above. Peabody gazed behind him at the deep pool of mud which, he now realized, had saved his life.

He looked up at the mountain and gulped again.

Somehow Sheriff Peabody had fallen over a thousand feet and yet had miraculously survived. He felt a pain on the back of his head and touched it with his bruised fingers.

A lump the size of a hen's egg pounded just behind his right ear.

He tried to check himself for broken bones but was still too dazed to know whether or not he was finding any. It seemed as if every part of his body was bruised but now he knew why.

His bloodshot eyes studied the rocky route that he must have either slid over or bounced off on his descent after being knocked from his saddle. Water and mud still flowed over it as it had done during the hours of darkness. That was why he was still alive, he thought.

Pushing himself away from the rocks, the sheriff staggered out into the muddy canyon, trying to see the trail upon which he prayed that his deputy was still in one piece. Shielding his eyes from the rain he stared up at the massive wall of rock. Then he spotted the horseman leading the pack-mule, far above him.

Tom was still OK, he sighed to himself. For a moment he thought about calling out to his friend but then realized that Tom had enough on his plate just negotiating the twisting slippery trail, without being startled by a ghost. For that was what the young deputy would think he was. After seeing him falling off the perilous trail, he must have resigned himself to his sheriff's death. Peabody knew that it was best that Tom continued to think that way until he reached the floor of the canyon.

Knowing that he had to try and think of what to do whilst waiting for his companion to reach him, the lawman tried to walk but felt sick. He rested against a massive boulder and then saw a sight which astounded him almost as much as his own survival.

His grey horse was standing less than fifty feet away from where he had woken up in the pool of mud. Peabody suddenly began to feel that his luck was still with him.

The sheriff put two fingers into his mouth

and whistled until the obedient grey trotted through the driving rain towards him.

Peabody grabbed the bridle of the horse and rested his temple against its nose.

'Good ol' Whiskey,' he muttered as the horse nodded up and down. 'I knew you'd not leave ya pal.'

Suddenly the lawman recalled whom he and his partner were chasing. His hand reached down for his gun but it was gone. The holster had been ripped from the belt somewhere during his unexpected fall.

A panic overwhelmed the sheriff. All his massive arsenal of weaponry and ammunition were strapped to the back of the mule high above him on the trail.

'Now we gotta wait until Tom gets down here, Whiskey,' the sheriff said into the ear of the horse. Then he noticed the massive buffalo gun tucked under the saddle of the grey. It was a huge weapon capable of hitting a bull off its feet from over a mile distant. He had not used the lethal weapon since his days of hunting buffalo for the bounty on their heads.

He checked his saddlebags and found the big handmade bullets inside.

For a moment he wondered if his theory of Zane Walker being in this unholy land was correct.

He got his answer quite unexpectedly when he heard the sound of a rifle shot echoing all around him. Without a second thought, Sheriff Peabody grabbed the horn of his saddle, stepped into his stirrup and mounted the grey.

Walker was here, he thought.

Peabody spurred the grey and headed off into the maze of canyons. He knew that he had no time to wait for his deputy to arrive with the arsenal of weapons and ammunition. He had to track Walker down.

Another shot rang out in the distance. The lawman wondered who the deadly outlaw was firing at. Whoever it was, he felt sorry for the critter.

SIXTEEN

Each of the five men dropped on to their stomachs into the muddy water and stared through the driving rain at the wall of solid granite that faced them. The canyon was narrow, and less than 500 feet in length but its walls towered higher than anything else any of the five had ever experienced, apart from the mesas back in the valley. The end of the canyon held a sight which was awesome. The rocks rose into a mountain that must be more than 1,000 feet high. It was rugged and easily climbed if there was no one taking pot shots at you, Slim thought. But Zane was up there and he was shooting.

The handsome cowboy lay in the mud holding his cocked Colt in his hand, watching the cave. Mist and sweeping rain filled the entire canyon and defied the rays of the sun to bring any heat into this strange place. Slim went to move his hand when his fingers felt something just beneath the water. He gripped it and pulled it up.

It was a human skull. He stared at the hole

in the top of it and knew that whoever this had once been, he or she had been clubbed to death. As he looked around them, he saw more and more of the spine-chilling objects piled against the canyon walls.

For the first time since they had entered the canyon, he knew why it had its unnerving name. There were skulls everywhere. Slim dropped the skull and then wiped his wet hand on his wet sleeve as if vainly attempting to rid it of some unseen horror.

This was a place where men had either been killed or the remnants of their bodies had been brought for some unthinkable reason. He felt his blood running cold.

Slim Walker narrowed his eyes and pulled the brim of his Stetson down. The rain pounded like war drums on to the battered hat, ran off the wide brim and dripped continuously. The cowboy was out of his depth and he knew it. This was his brother's game and Slim knew that compared to his twin, he was a mere amateur.

The mud-splattered face turned and looked at the three younger Apache braves as they crawled to cover beside the array of boulders which littered the floor of the canyon. They were as terrified as he was and it showed. Slim waved a hand at them and nodded. They clutched their bows and arrows and waited for their chief to instruct them.

Slim had seen the rifle barrel poke through the curtain of water that flowed over the entrance of the cave set high on the end wall of the dead-end canyon. It had fired blindly but the shots had still come too close for comfort. Slim swallowed hard and scrambled to the side of Heronis.

Neither man had spoken since entering Skull Canyon as they tried to work out how they could get close enough to the massive mountain face to have a hope of even seeing Zane. Slim wondered whether he ought to shoot back but knew that his .45 did not have the lethal range of the Winchester. Nor did the arrows of his trusting friends.

He was thankful that the rain was giving them cover but knew that the storm would not last indefinitely.

They had to make a move soon if they were to have a remote chance of getting the drop on Zane. But as usual, his identical brother was holding all the cards. He had chosen his hideout well and would be able to pick them all off like sitting ducks once the rain ceased.

Slim bit his lip and looked up at the wall

of rocks beside Heronis and himself. The granite rocks were huge but easily climbed if a man had good reason to do so, and he had more than enough reasons to do so.

Without knowing exactly why, Slim reached into his back pocket, dragged the six bullets out and handed them to the Apache chieftain. Then he unbuckled his gunbelt and gave that to Heronis as well. Finally he placed the Colt into the weathered hands and smiled.

'What are you doing, Slim?' the chief asked.

Slim removed his hat and placed it on the Indian's head. He ran his fingers through his hair until it was off his face.

'I'm gonna try and get close to Zane and if I have half a chance, I'll jump the critter.'

Heronis offered the pistol back to the cowboy.

'You need this, my friend. This man might be your brother but he will kill you quickly if he get a chance. You need gun to shoot him.'

Slim rose to his feet and studied the rocks beside them.

'I've known for a long time that I could never kill him or anyone else for that matter. The gun will slow me down.'

'But he will shoot you, Slim.' The face of Heronis was grim with concern.

Slim patted the Indian's wet shoulder.

'Give me cover. You just shoot at that cave entrance every few minutes and that'll distract him. Leastways, I sure hope it does.'

Before the Apache could speak again, Slim Walker had climbed up the huge rockface. Heronis gripped the gun in his hand and watched as the young cowboy moved steadily upward through the mist as rain continued to pour down. He knew that Slim was going to try and make his way across the side walls of the canyon until he reached the huge mountain where Zane was secreted. The old Indian felt his heart sink as another massive explosion of thunder deafened them.

Then the sky lit up as lightning flashed across the sky above them. Heronis glanced above him but could no longer see where his young friend was. He knew that it was now up to the agility of the cowboy to get close to the man brandishing the long-barrelled carbine. Getting the attention of his followers, the Apache chief spoke to his three young braves with his hands. They understood his commands and moved instantly forward from one boulder to the next. They had managed to close the distance between themselves and the rifleman but were still too far away for their arrows to bridge the gap.

Heronis then did the same. He knew they had to try and get into range if they were going to be able to help Slim and have any chance of hitting Zane with their arrows or the bullets in the pistol.

A fork of lightning branched down from the angry black clouds and hit the foot of the mountain where Zane's mount was tethered. The animal jumped off the ground as fragments of rubble showed over it, but it could not break free from where it had been secured by the tightly knotted reins.

Zane Walker cranked the mechanism of his Winchester, moved to the corner of the cave entrance and stared down on to Skull Canyon from his high vantage point. He had already fired two bullets down at the ghostlike shadows which he had seen moving through the misty rain, but knew that he had not yet killed anyone.

The deadly outlaw cursed the ceaseless rain for obscuring his targets from his keen eyes. He could see them moving around down there in the rising mist of the continuous downpour, but never clearly enough to get an accurate shot off. The water flowed over the mouth of the cave like a waterfall, hampering his ability to slay the uninvited intruders.

Zane's hat-brim and shirt sleeves were soaked as he aimed the lethal carbine down at the ground below him. He wanted to kill and nothing else could ever satisfy the hunger inside his belly. He was like an animal craving its prey. Only the taste of his victims' blood would satisfy him now.

Once again he fired.

Once more, he missed.

The anger inside him began to boil over. He knew that whoever they were, they were getting closer, yet he was unable to pick them off. The sky flashed and lightning blinded him temporarily, forcing him away from the mouth of his cave. He rubbed his eyes and cursed loudly before moving to the other side of the cave entrance. He pushed himself up against the wall of wet stone as he cocked the rifle again.

The spent bullet-casing flashed past his face as he tried once more to find a target worthy of his talents.

The driving rain and brilliant sun that faced him made it impossible to see anything clearly. He screwed up his eyes and, trying to defy the elements themselves, he fired his rifle.

He was confused.

How many of them were there?

He had counted three already but knew that there must be more. He could sense it with every ounce of his deadly killer's instincts.

Who were they? he wondered as he squeezed the Winchester's trigger again.

His bullet flashed through the rain like a firefly. Zane's keen ears managed to hear the bullet bouncing off the rocks below him.

Once again he primed the Winchester.

Who were they?

Was this a posse?

There had never been a posse with enough nerve to enter the vast valley of the mesas before. None that could have tracked him to Skull Canyon, anyway.

If it was a posse, how could they have found his hiding-place in this storm? The ground was awash and all tracks had been obliterated. So who were these fools?

Again he fired down into the canyon and cranked the lever of his rifle.

A haunting thought crept into his mind. Could this be Slim down there? If so, who was with him?

But Slim was dead! Zane recalled seeing his brother falling from the back of his horse when he had opened up with his trusty carbine back in the sun-baked valley.

Slim must be dead, he thought. He could not have missed him from that range. Then Zane remembered the blistering heat haze that had troubled him when he had lain in wait for his twin brother.

For more than two hours he had patiently bided his time waiting for Slim to ride into range as a million ants had crawled over his body, gnawing at his flesh. The heat had been so intense in the huge valley that he had not seen Slim's shimmering image at first.

Zane recalled how he had allowed Slim to get far closer to him than he would normally have had to because of the heat vapours that rose off the floor of the valley. But when he had unleashed his lethal fury, he had seen him fall.

Could he have missed?

Doubts began to fester in the brain of the outlaw.

A million questions screamed above the sound of the rain that continued to pour down from the storm clouds above him. The outlaw screwed his eyes up again and tried to get a bead on at least one of them.

It was impossible.

How could he shoot what he could hardly see?

Zane knew that he had to get out into the open away from the flowing water that poured over the entrance to his secret hiding-place. The morning sunlight was blinding his every attempt at killing the men who had invaded Skull Canyon.

There was no way he could get a clear shot from within the cave itself.

He had a decision to make.

Did he remain inside this place and wait for them to slowly advance on him? Or did he strike out and try and pick them off one by one in the open?

There was no other way than to pick them off if he wanted to kill them, and he wanted to kill them real bad.

Zane fired and then lowered his rifle and tried to hear if anyone out there was talking. There were no words being spoken.

He inhaled deeply.

'Is that you, Slim?' There was a desperation in the voice of the outlaw. 'Slim?'

There was no reply.

Zane Walker lifted the rifle, cocked it and

fired again and again until the hammer of the Winchester fell on to an empty chamber. If it was his brother down there, he was not giving away his position, the fuming outlaw thought. Slim did not know much but he knew enough not to give his deadly twin something to home his rifle sights on.

Zane was convinced that Slim must be one of the men down in the canyon. He just had to be.

The snorting killer returned to his bags and dragged out a box of rifle bullets and pulled its lid off. He snatched a handful of the shells.

One by one he pushed the bullets into the rifle and talked to himself. But his words meant nothing. For the only thing he said was the name of his brother. He repeated the name with every one of the bullets that he pushed into the rifle's magazine.

When the weapon was loaded he moved back to the flowing water which was like a liquid curtain and then forced his way out into the daylight.

Once again he started firing the rifle down into the belly of Skull Canyon.

There was hatred in every single shot.

SEVENTEEN

Every rifle shot drew the bruised and battered lawman closer to the wanted man he sought. Zane Walker was a valuable prize that the sheriff did not want to miss out on. He was worth more than all of the other hunted outlaws Peabody had tracked down, put together.

Even injured the lawman was unable to resist riding towards the sound of the rifle shots that echoed all around him. He was being drawn like a moth to a flame, but unlike a moth, the sheriff knew how dangerous his chosen flame was.

He had started out slowly on his grey not knowing what lay ahead of him in the maze of narrow corridors of solid stone, but now he found that he was spurring the mount.

Marvin Peabody knew that there could only be one man capable of unleashing so much venomous lead in such a short period of time.

Zane Walker!

The sheriff knew that the outlaw was close

and he wanted him in the sights of his trusty buffalo gun. With every stride that his grey took, the rifle shots had grown louder. He urged the horse on and on without even considering what he would do should he run into the ruthless outlaw around any of the natural stone corners.

As the horse reached its best pace, the lawman had pulled the huge buffalo gun from its custom-made scabbard and laid it across his saddle horn. He knew that this was not the ideal weapon to try and bring down anything smaller than the massive beasts it was designed to fell, but he had little choice.

Peabody drove the animal on along the muddy trail and knew that it would obey his every demand. This was a horse that would gallop until its heart exploded, if asked to do so.

The lawman reined in as a mighty bolt of lightning cut through the driving rain ahead of him and blasted the side off a huge wall of granite.

Debris showered over the horse and rider as the stench of burning filled the nostrils of both man and beast. The sheriff steadied the grey just long enough to hear the next of the rifle shots. He spun his mount around and stood in his stirrups.

'Hear that, Whiskey? That bastard is darn close!' he said to the nervous horse. Peabody had noticed a taste in his mouth a few miles back and it lingered. He spat and knew that it was blood that had left his mouth. For the first time since he had woken up at the foot of the mountain trail, he realized that he had internal injuries. He felt blood in his mouth again and spat once more. His free hand searched in his deep wet pockets for his chewing-tobacco and found the large block of black Virginian Best. He peeled the silver paper off it and bit off a huge chunk and started chewing. The flavour disguised the taste of the blood that kept finding its way into his throat. He spat again and smiled.

He had been injured many times before and it did not trouble him. He knew that the worst thing that could happen to a man who wore a star on his chest was getting himself killed.

Anything less was not worth fretting over.

Peabody spun the horse around again when a thunderclap rocked the ground beneath them. Sheriff Peabody could see little through the rain and the walls of rock that surrounded him, but thought he knew roughly where the rifleman must be.

As he managed to get the horse moving again, he began to recall the small series of canyons that lay about a mile ahead of him. It had been years since he had last ventured this deep into the deadly land, but he knew exactly where they were.

Zane Walker was doing battle with somebody in one of those canyons, he thought. It was time for the law to step in.

The grey began to make pace again with its master stood high in his stirrups above the neck of the powerful horse. With one hand on the massive buffalo gun and the other gripping the reins, the sheriff rode on toward the canyons.

One of which was the mysterious Skull Canyon!

EIGHTEEN

None of the four startled Apaches had expected to see Zane Walker burst out from his sanctuary and start shooting down at them in the raging storm, but there he was standing squarely on the high ledge firing his Winchester.

The outlaw seemed crazed. A soul at odds with the very elements themselves. This had been his secret place and now it had been violated. Zane seemed not only to be shooting down into the canyon at the fleeting images of those beneath him, but also at the very storm clouds above his head.

The Apaches had seen many things in their pitiful existences but they had never witnessed anything like this before. The chief wondered if the man thought that they were unarmed or perhaps that he was somehow immortal.

Or both.

Even though startled, Heronis knew that he had to try and divert the lethal gunman's attention quickly from his three young braves and Slim Walker who was somewhere high up on the cliff face making his way towards the cave. If he did not, one or all of them would soon fall victim to the rifle bullets spewing from the long Winchester barrel.

The Apache chief raised the Colt .45, stared down its length through the sights and then squeezed its wet trigger. The handgun kicked hard in the hand that had never before used one of these weapons.

The bullet fell short of its target but served its purpose and made Zane suddenly aware that the men below him were indeed armed.

The outlaw dropped to his knees and stared hard through the driving rain and blinding sunshine that somehow managed to filter its rays into the canyon beneath the raging storm clouds.

'Is that you, Slim?' Zane screamed out. Again there was no reply.

Suddenly another bullet was fired from the Colt and this time Zane caught sight of the tell-tale gunsmoke leaving its barrel from below the high rocky ledge.

Faster than a heartbeat, Zane cranked the rifle's lever and fired down at Heronis. The Winchester bullet ricocheted off the boulder behind which the chief was kneeling and made him delay his third shot. Another vicious shot skimmed through the air and took the hat off the Apache chief's head. Heronis glanced across at his three warriors and told them, with his intricate hand signals, to stay exactly where they were.

Zane Walker got back to his feet but stayed low and moved several yards to his left, trying to see if it were possible to get an accurate shot at the man who was well hidden. His eyes narrowed as he tried to see through the waves of misty rain between himself and his target. He cocked the Winchester and expelled its spent shell.

The outlaw raised the rifle to his shoulder again, held his breath and then fired.

The bullet tore through the leg of the kneeling Indian chief and sent him reeling closer to the wall of solid rock. Heronis was wounded, yet knew that the survival of his companions rested in his hands. Forcing himself upright and gritting his teeth, he aimed the pistol straight up in the air and squeezed its trigger.

The shot startled the outlaw enough to make him drop back on to one knee. His eyes searched around the rocks beneath his high perch, trying to work out if the shot had come from the same pistol as the previous ones or from the gun of one of the other intruders to his hiding-place.

Now the outlaw was losing his confidence. Maybe they were all well-armed and had just been luring him out of the safety of his cave.

Zane pushed the rifle lever down and then hauled it back up once more. The sky erupted above his head and made him cower in stunned shock as everything within Skull Canyon shook, including the mountain he was standing upon. This was the first time he had been outside his cave when the ear-splitting noise of the storm had made its power felt.

Zane Walker did not like the experience. Stumbling over the shaking ledge, he desperately tried to return to his sanctuary when the entire sky lit up with a series of brilliant lightning flashes.

The light was so bright that it diminished the power of the morning sun. The outlaw yelled in pain and clutched his eyes as he fell forward. For a few endless moments, he could see nothing but the white that had burned the pupils of his eyes.

Zane found himself on his knees waiting for his vision to be returned to him.

Noticing the distress that their evil prey

was in, Heronis signalled his braves to advance as he too ran from behind the boulder. The four Apaches moved swiftly through the ceaseless rain until they were almost at the foot of the mighty mountainside.

Heronis signalled his men and they trained their weaponry on the high ledge above them. Now they were well within range and were going to take full advantage of that precious fact.

Before Zane Walker had managed to regain his sight he heard the shots coming at him far below. He turned and lifted his rifle to his shoulder as a bullet passed close enough to his head to hit the brim of his hat.

He felt it being torn from his head and knew that the tables had been turned.

The outlaw was shocked when he saw his Stetson floating down into the canyon. He fell on to his belly and tried to work out what was happening.

Was this another of the intruders?

Did they all have guns?

Was Slim one of them?

Who and where were they?

His mind raced. Slowly Zane crawled towards the rim of the ledge and peered down. Suddenly he saw someone standing up from behind a boulder. The outlaw raised the barrel of his rifle. At the same moment an arrow came within inches of hitting him.

The arrow had been shot from the opposite side of the canyon where he had seen the man. When his attention went back to Heronis he saw and heard the Colt .45 being fired again.

He tried to duck but no man could move faster than a bullet once the gun hammer had sent it on its journey.

The bullet ripped through the shoulder-padding of his jacket and he felt his skin burning. He had been winged.

Zane Walker moved away from the edge of the rim and realized that they were Apaches.

The deadly outlaw knew that he had killed enough of them in the past to warrant their seeking vengeance and striking back, but why now?

Why had they waited so long?

What had given them the courage to attack him now?

Or was it who?

Another arrow flew over him and shattered against the mountain wall behind him. Zane moved even further away from the edge of the rim. He was breathing hard now as he felt blood trickling down inside his sleeve from the graze on his shoulder. He had heard many tales of what these nomadic people did to their enemies once they captured them. He prayed the stories were not true.

For years Zane Walker had always been the victor in all his fights because he had usually started them. The element of surprise had destroyed many a better gunman. He had struck with lethal venom and destroyed all who stood in his way. It was easy to kill someone who had no idea that he was about to become your next victim and be destroyed.

The innocent never defend themselves because they imagine they are safe. If all men were sane, that would be true. But men like Zane Walker were not blessed with the morality of the majority of his fellow men.

His was a simple philosophy, do unto others before they do it to you. Until now, it had worked.

This was not the sort of fight he was used to. This one was very, very different. This time his enemies were bringing the battle to his doorstep and he did not like it. They had the advantage. Now he was beginning to realize what it felt like to be on the receiving end of such anger.

Yet even now he could not accept that he had ever done anything wrong. It was others who were misguided. It was never his fault.

The sky rumbled angrily again and made him feel even more nervous. Zane raised his rifle and tried to fire down at his hidden enemies, but then felt the hammer striking an empty bullet magazine. His eyes flashed over at the cave. He had to get back there to reload the Winchester, he thought.

Another flash of lightning above him made his heart skip a beat. Were the very elements themselves joining forces with his foes?

An arrow caught the barrel of his rifle and tore it from his hands. He watched helplessly as it fell into the canyon.

Now his mind was made up, he would go back into the cave and wait for the Apaches to come after him. He would use his lethal Colt .45 to cut them down, one by one.

Zane decided to run as fast as his legs would take him, back to the cave along the wet, narrow, cliff ledge. If he was quick enough, the Indians would not even see him through the driving rain.

He turned and began to ready himself. It was only a matter of a dozen yards or even less to safety, but now arrows and bullets were flying across his chosen path.

But Zane had faced worse and managed to come out on top.

Then looking up, he saw the familiar figure of the tall man moving down off the huge granite wall towards him until they both shared the same slippery ledge.

The arrows and bullets ceased.

Zane Walker rubbed the rainwater from his eyes. The face which was identical to his own handsome image was staring silently at him.

'Slim!'

NINETEEN

Slim Walker had not stopped his intrepid climb across the top of the canyon wall for a single second. It had not been an easy task with the raging storm overhead. The rocks were wet and slippery and yet he had made good progress during the exchange of fire between his brother and the four ill-equipped Apache warriors far below him. Although totally unarmed, Slim had not faltered in his determined advance up and across the canyon walls toward the mountain.

His blood had run cold when he had seen how strangely his brother was acting. Although still the exact duplicate of himself in features, Zane now seemed utterly deranged. The cowboy did not recognize any of the actions coming from his twin. Had all the years of brutal slayings finally twisted the evil brain inside Zane's head?

This was not the same man whom the cowboy had last met years earlier. This was a monster who simply resembled himself, Slim thought as he stared at Zane.

Their eyes were locked on to one another's. Neither man dared to blink in case they gave an advantage to the other.

Now standing face to face with the brother he had chased for over a hundred miles, Slim could not bring himself to judge the cruel man. He moved cautiously toward the crazed outlaw who had brought so much pain to so many innocent souls. He knew that it was up to him to try and stop him.

But how?

'I knew it was you,' Zane snarled, taking several steps closer to the one man he hated more than all the others he had encountered and killed over the years. 'I felt you out here in the rain, Slim. I could smell your yellow streak.'

The cowboy looked down and took another step forward.

'I knew that you would sense me getting closer and closer, Zane.'

The outlaw rested the palm of his left hand on the notched gun grip and smiled. It was the smile of a man considering how and when to kill.

'I thought that you were dead back at the valley, Slim.'

Slim stared at the pair of lethal guns that sat in their holsters on the hips of his twin.

He knew, however, that it was only the left one he had to be concerned about. Zane had many skills but he had never been able to use his right hand, unlike himself.

'You killed my horse, Zane. It was a darn good horse.'

'I was aiming at you.' The outlaw stared through the driving rain at the eyes of his mirror image but there was little if any reaction to the statement.

'I already figured that out, Zane.' Slim sighed. 'Darn shame though. This ain't the sort of place that treats a man on foot too kindly.'

'My black stallion would never have bin caught by that two-dollar nag of yours, Slim.' There was a smugness in the tone of the voice. A mocking that was aimed at the soul of the slightly older Walker brother. 'When you got money like me, you can buy yourself all sorts of real expensive things. But then, you probably don't understand. You being a pig-farmer and such.'

Slim carefully walked past the flowing water that marked the entrance to the cave and continued slowly towards his brother without a glimmer of expression on his face.

'I'm no pig-farmer. I'm a cattle-rancher like our pa was and you know it. I might be poor but I ain't gone around killing folks like you.'

Zane looked defiant. 'That's 'coz you're a coward. There ain't a bone in that spine of yours and you know it.'

'I can sleep at night.'

'So can I. I'm rich, Slim.' Zane laughed as he rested his other hand on the right gun-grip. 'That cave is full of my loot. I must have me ten thousand dollars in there in gold coin and paper money. What have you got besides blisters on your butt? You ain't got nothing at all. Not even a horse anymore.'

Slim stopped his advance and studied the hands of his twin. So far they had not flicked the small leather safety loops off the gun hammers. But the thumbs were twitching in readiness to do so.

'You're dead right. I ain't got me nothing. I owe the bank fifty bucks and yet I don't hide away in no darn cave like some darn grizzly bear.'

Zane inhaled deeply.

'You're still a coward.'

'How do you reckon on that?' Slim wiped the rain off his face and tried not to dwell on the fact that at any moment the pair of Colt .45s might come bursting from their holsters and start spitting lead.

'All the months you've been dogging my trail and you ain't once tried to shoot me, Slim.' Zane grinned and tilted his head. 'Was you scared?'

Slim wondered whether he could possibly get the better of this monster, who was like a stranger to him.

'Nope. You were just never in range of my sixgun, Zane.'

'But if'n I had been in range, would you have shot me?'

'If I'd had a rifle, I might have taken a shot.'

Zane kicked at the mud at his feet and bit his lip. 'How come you decided to come after me, Slim? Many have tried but none of the bastards ever got close. I've lost count of how many men I've sent to their graves.'

Slim nodded.

'I reckon the thought passed through my mind once or twice but I just had to keep trailing you.'

'Why?'

'Reckon it's my job. There ain't nobody else.'

'But would you kill me?' Zane doubted it. 'A man who could never bring himself to go hunting and would throw up if he even saw

146

a critter shot, would somehow be able to try and kill his own brother?'

Slim knew that they were now a mere ten feet apart. He wondered if it were possible to bridge that distance before Zane could draw that lethal pistol from the left holster. His brother was the fastest man with a gun that he had ever seen and he doubted that he had lost any of his skill over the years since their last meeting.

'I reckon you're right again, Zane.' Slim shrugged and edged a few inches forward. 'I could never kill you but I knew that you would kill me, though, when the mood took you. I'm kinda surprised that you ain't done for me already.'

Zane laughed.

'There's still time, big brother.'

Slim watched in silent horror as he saw Zane's left thumb flick the safety loop off the gun hammer. Yet his deadly brother stared down at the canyon as if he had done nothing at all. Slim knew this was his way of distracting his prey.

'Are them Injuns with you?' Zane asked.

'Yep,' Slim replied.

'How come?' The outlaw could not understand. 'I don't know why you've teamed up with a bunch of savages.'

Slim kept his eyes on the hands of his brother, knowing that there would be warning when they went into action. 'Them so-called savages saved my life.'

Zane raised an eyebrow and returned his eyes to his twin brother. There was curiosity etched in his expression. In his entire life he had never done one kind thing for anyone. It was something that was totally alien to his nature.

'They did? When?'

'After some *hombre* shot my horse out from under me.'

Zane laughed.

'I still can't believe that I missed you. You must be blessed with some of my good luck.'

Slim knew he had to get just a little closer. 'You came close enough to killing me.'

'But not quite close enough to stop you following me.' The outlaw was still grinning. 'You loco or something?'

'Yep. I sure must be,' Slim admitted. 'After all it must be the act of a crazy person to dog the tail of a killer, even if he is blood kin.'

'You realize that I gotta kill you and then finish off them redskins, don't you?' The palm of Zane's left hand was moving back and forth over the wooden gun-grip as he spoke.

'I figured as much.'

'Ain't nothin' personal, Slim. I just gotta protect my hideout. I got me too much loot stashed away in that cave to let outsiders learn about it.'

Suddenly the rain began to ease up noticeably and both men looked up at the sky at precisely the same moment. The cowboy knew that if he was going to make an attempt at jumping his brother, it had better be pretty soon. Time was running out for him fast. Slim knew how his brother thought and could read his every evil thought. Zane was just making small talk until he felt the inescapable desire to draw his weapon and squeeze its trigger.

The sky above them erupted again. It felt as if a stick of dynamite had exploded directly above the two brothers. Both men felt the sheer force pressing down on their bedraggled shoulders as the entire mountain appeared to rock beneath their boots.

Sheet lightning flashed across the heavens in bursts of electrical power neither man had ever experienced before.

Slim Walker noticed that it was his brother who seemed the more alarmed of the pair.

He seemed to be frozen in shock as all around them the air crackled furiously.

'The Apache down there are only the scouting party, Zane,' Slim lied to his terrified brother. 'There's a whole bunch of the critters outside Skull Canyon.'

The outlaw suddenly looked straight at the cowboy.

'How did you know that I call this place Skull Canyon?'

'I read your mind, Zane.'

The outlaw pointed a long finger at his brother. 'Don't start that crap about being able to read my mind again, Slim. We ain't kids no more. That's just a lot of hogwash and you know it.'

Slim knew that his brother was now totally confused. Zane had never been at ease with anything he could not kill and there was no way that he could destroy the storm above them.

'There are a dozen more Apaches outside the canyon,' Slim said, watching the reaction his words had on the face of his twin brother.

Zane forced a grin.

'Now you don't think I'm gonna fall for that one, do you?'

Slim shrugged.

'I really don't care if you believe me or

not. It ain't my scalp that they'll be lifting.'

The outlaw felt his entire body shake as another thunderclap tore through the clouds above them. He knew that his unease had been witnessed by Slim and he was angry. 'Apache don't scare me, Slim.'

'If I was in your boots, they wouldn't scare me if I had a Winchester.' Slim wiped the rain from his face and studied his brother's expression closely. 'Where is your rifle, anyway?'

Zane Walker gritted his teeth as he recalled the arrow plucking his trusty carbine from his grip only minutes earlier.

'I don't need no rifle to polish off a bunch of redskins. I got me two Colts and they'll do just dandy.'

'But how are you going to get out of here afterwards?' The cowboy inched closer.

'On my horse. How else?'

Slim shook his head and decided to add fuel to Zane's uncertainty.

'Them Apache are down there with your prized stallion right now.'

Zane moved to the very edge of the ledge and looked down. He could not see his mount from this place. For the first time since his reunion with the brother he had hated for his entire life, he was worried.

The outlaw swung around and walked closer to Slim. He pointed a finger and screamed.

'They wouldn't hurt my stallion.'

'Angry folks are inclined to do the most unexpected things, Zane.' Slim knew that he was now less than eight feet from his troubled sibling. 'Your problem is that they ain't just angry, they're also starving. Your big black stallion would fill a lotta bellies back in their camp.'

'They wouldn't kill and eat my horse. That's loco.'

'What if they do? How in tarnation are you gonna get out of this land on foot? I almost died after being out on that valley floor for just a few hours.'

'Shut ya damn mouth!' Zane had heard enough.

Slim dropped his shoulder and charged across the ledge. With each stride he saw his brother's hand getting closer to the gun grip of the Colt on his left hip.

The palm of Zane's left hand pushed the gun hammer back until it locked into position, whilst his fingers lifted the weapon from the holster and began to raise its barrel.

Zane Walker had slapped and drawn the

.45 in a mere heartbeat.

Slim's shoulder hit his brother squarely, then the cowboy heard and felt the venom of the pistol as it fired.

TWENTY

Heronis stood beside his three Apache braves watching the battle above them. He had held his faithful followers in check and stopped them from using their deadly bows and arrows whilst Slim was so close to his twin brother on the ledge above them.

Now the chief's heart pounded like the ancient drums of his noble people. Had he made a mistake which would cause the death of the quiet young cowboy he had rescued?

The pistol in Zane Walker's hand had fired twice and yet the two men still wrestled on the high ledge. The Indian chief looked up in horror, knowing that he and his young followers were well within range for their arrows and bullets to kill the evil outlaw who had so callously destroyed so many of his tribe.

The rain no longer fell into their hooded eyes but the deadly storm had not finished with Skull Canyon yet. Ripples of lightning traced through the clouds as if following the thunder which still warned of its terrifying power.

Heronis was restless and wounded but he knew he had not mastered the Colt .45 he held in his hand well enough to even dare using it now. He could not do anything to assist the brave cowboy who battled with his own personal demon up on the mountain. The Apache chief raised his hand to his men telling them to lower their bows.

The two men above them were locked in a fight that made it impossible to be certain of hitting the right one. All Heronis and his three open-mouthed warriors could do was simply stand and watch.

Sheriff Marvin Peabody had encountered the peaceful Apaches before but was still taken aback when he rode his grey in through the narrow neck of Skull Canyon, at the sight before him. The four Indians looked more dead than alive. Their emaciated bodies were evidence that they were slowly starving in this harrowing land of red sand and granite mesas. It had been the five thin painted ponies that had led the injured lawman to this place but he was still shocked at what met his eyes.

Hauling in his reins Peabody allowed his

bedraggled mount to walk slowly towards the four warriors. Heronis nodded at the man whom he remembered meeting several years earlier. The sheriff dismounted and spat at the ground before moving to the side of the chief.

Then his eyes drifted up at the mountain before them where the young braves were pointing. The sight that confronted him stunned the wily old sheriff. Even from where they stood it was clear that the outlaw Peabody had sought was fighting hand to hand on a narrow ledge. Then the lawman's jaw dropped when he caught sight of the two faces.

Both of them belonged to the crumpled Wanted poster in his pocket. They were both the face of Zane Walker.

With every ounce of his deadly viciousness, the ruthless outlaw kicked his brother repeatedly in the ribs and yet could not break free from the hands that gripped his own. Slim held the left wrist of Zane and used his years of experience tackling half-ton mavericks to keep the lethal pistol from aiming anywhere near him.

Both men crashed into the mountain wall. The gun fired again and gunpowder burned into their faces as they rolled over the wall of solid rock. Zane had tried to pull his other gun from its holster but felt the strong grip of his brother's left hand holding his weaker arm well away from the wooden notched gun-grip.

For the first time since the pair were children, they were fighting with the only thing they possessed: their strength. And for the first time since those far-off days, it was Slim who was the stronger.

The tables had been turned full circle because it was Slim who had worked hard roping and branding steers, whilst his twin had merely roamed the West doing nothing more energetic than using his gun to kill anyone who got in his way.

Zane thrust his pointed boot into his brother's shin and they started to fall sideways. Both men fell heavily on to the ledge and the pistol fired again. A bullet passed over Slim's right shoulder but he did not release his vicelike grip on his brother's arms. A knee came up and caught the cowboy in his ribs, but he still held on.

Zane twisted and turned but was hampered by his heavy wet jacket. With each movement he could feel the blood from his wounded shoulder trickling down inside his shirt. But the outlaw was not ready to quit just yet.

He had summoned death to his aid many times and it had never let him down yet. All he required was half a chance and he would put a bullet through his brother's head or heart.

Zane lay beneath his brother and gritted his teeth. He could see that this fight was not taking as much out of Slim as it was out of him. He was panting and knew that he had to do something fast if he were ever going to escape from this man and this place. The outlaw had made a mistake and talked when he should have just started shooting.

It was an error that Zane vowed to remedy.

Using every fragment of power he had in his neck muscles, Zane arched his body and then head-butted Slim in the face. Blood spattered from the bridge of the cowboy's nose as the skin split apart under the impact of the unexpected blow.

For a split second, the outlaw felt Slim go suddenly limp above him.

Zane only required that mere second to heave the stunned body off his own. The senseless cowboy fell heavily and slid across the slippery surface. Zane lifted his Colt, cocked its hammer and squeezed the trigger. The bullet missed its target by a fraction of an inch as Slim tumbled off the ledge and rolled down over the uneven rocks until he landed on a boulder that jutted out from the side of the mountain.

Below them, Heronis told his braves to prime their bows as Sheriff Peabody hauled the large buffalo gun off the brow of his saddle.

The impact seemed to awaken Slim and he blinked hard until he could see clearly again. On the canyon floor, Slim saw the four Indians and the man with the massive rifle, which was unlike any he had seen before. Their faces were grim and anxious.

He soon figured out why.

Spinning around on the boulder and looking back up at the ledge he saw Zane staggering to his feet with the deadly Colt in his hand. The outlaw went to move to the rim of the narrow ledge when a volley of arrows sent him reeling backwards.

Zane fired wildly until his hammer fell on spent shells. He went to move back towards the cave but a deafening blast from the buffalo gun made him duck. A huge chunk of the rock was torn off the boulders beside him.

Zane stared at the smouldering gash in the granite and swallowed hard. He had no idea what sort of weapon could do that kind of damage and was in no hurry to find out.

Slim began to climb up the sheer face of the mountainside as if he knew that only he could put a stop to this once and for all time. Somehow he had to find a way of getting the better of his evil *doppelgänger*. Even if it meant sacrificing his own life, he had to stop Zane here.

With the agility of a man used to physical labours, the cowboy quickly reached the ledge once more. He saw the panic in his brother's face as he reappeared over the rocky rim.

Zane's face looked as if he had seen a ghost. He yelled out in terrified anger and threw his pistol straight at his brother as the cowboy clawed his way back on to the wet ledge.

The gun caught him across the right side of his temple but did not slow Slim's progress. The cowboy clambered to his feet again and watched as Zane lunged at him once more. Slim blocked the left hook with his forearm and slammed a short accurate right to the jaw.

He watched as Zane stumbled backwards and hit the uneven rocky side of the mountain hard. The two men stared into each other's eyes as if searching for each other's souls.

Blood trickled freely from Zane's mouth as a twisted grin defied Slim to keep coming. The cowboy moved in fast and went to throw another clenched right fist at the smiling face but Zane kicked out and caught Slim low. It was as if every ounce of wind had been dragged from his body.

The cowboy buckled and felt a solid left hook catching the side of his own bleeding face. He fell forward and grabbed out at the legs before him.

A knee came up and tossed Slim's head back.

Both men fell to their knees but it was Zane who now seemed to have the upper hand. Blows rained into the face of the winded cowboy but he held on for dear life. Slim knew that he had to absorb the vicious onslaught until it was his turn to strike out again.

Zane's hand reached for the pistol on his right hip but Slim managed to catch the outlaw with a swift uppercut.

The sound of teeth cracking inside Zane's mouth filled the air as they scrambled desperately to their feet again. Slim was blowing hard and feeling his strength slowly returning to his battered body.

He knew that he had to hang on and somehow stop his brother's remaining handgun from reaching the deadly accurate left hand.

Leaping with all his might, Slim pressed his forearm across the throat of his twin and pushed his head back against the wall of hard rock. Yet before either man could wield their next blow, another explosion of angry thunder shook the mountain as if it were a rag doll.

The whole mountain seemed to shudder.

The cowboy felt his feet slip from under him and he landed hard on his knees. Zane went to reach for his gun but could not find its grip with Slim dragging at his wet jacket and ankle. The outlaw kicked out, swiftly turned and started to climb up the rockface away from the brother he had underestimated and was beginning to fear.

Slim shook the blood from his face and clawed his way back to his feet. He lunged out and grabbed at the boot of his brother's trailing leg as he climbed up the rugged side of the high mountain. The razor-sharp edge of the spurs forced him to release his grip. Slim pulled his bleeding hand back and looked at the deep gash across the knuckles. Instinctively, Slim put the hand to his lips and sucked the blood as he watched Zane getting further and further away from him.

Whether Zane was fleeing him or just trying to get out of range of the Apache arrows, Slim could only guess. Perhaps in the sick mind of the outlaw, Zane actually thought that he could hide up in the rocks until darkness came again over Skull Canyon and then make his way back down and kill them all.

Whatever the reason for Zane's choosing to climb, Slim Walker knew that there was no escape where his brother was heading. He also knew that their fight was still not over and it would not be until one or both of them was dead.

Mustering all his gritty determination, the battered and bleeding cowboy managed to get a firm handhold and started up after him.

For more than five minutes, Slim carefully ascended the wet rockface in pursuit of his sibling. Never once taking his eyes from the figure above him, the tired cattleman found hand-and footholds; he started to close the gap between them.

Zane Walker suddenly realized that he was running out of mountain to climb. There was a small ledge ten or twenty feet above him but beyond that point he knew that there was no way for him to climb any higher. The outlaw knew that if he could reach the ledge he could rest and then pick off his brother.

But Zane was now moving ever more slowly. The thick water-sodden jacket hung heavily on him, allowing Slim to come nearer to him with every passing second. Zane looked around but knew that there were no safe options open to him, the higher up the mountain the outlaw got, the more likely he was to be either caught or trapped.

He had thought that he could climb over the jagged peak and find refuge in another canyon, but now realized that this was impossible; he would have to stop and fight his way back down the almost sheer rockface.

Slim stopped and watched as his brother rested a mere twenty feet above him. For a moment he wondered what Zane was doing as he lay against the wall of granite with his high-heeled toe-caps balanced on a sliver of rock that was less than two inches in width.

Then the cowboy realized that his twin was pulling off the heavy jacket that had been weighing him down. Slim bit his lip and tasted the blood that was running down the gashes in his tanned face.

Even now, after all he had suffered at the hands of his cold-hearted identical brother, the cowboy found himself holding his breath in case Zane fell from his precarious perch. Slim could still not hate him.

The ruthless Zane had less compassion in his dark soul. He removed his wet coat, held it by its sodden sleeve and stared down at his brother below him.

'You still dodging my tail, brother?' Zane called out.

Slim looked up. 'Yep. I'm still here.'

They were at least a hundred feet above the ridge near the cave and probably twice that distance from the canyon floor but neither man seemed to notice. All they could see was each other and the distance between them.

Zane dangled the wet heavy jacket directly above where his brother was resting on the side of the rockface.

Slim could hear the laughter above him. It was a crazed mocking laughter that chilled the bones of the cowboy. Then he saw Zane releasing his grip on the jacket.

'*Adios*, Slim!'

It fell like a lead weight straight down at Slim.

The cowboy felt the heavy wet coat hit

him hard. For one terrifying second, he thought that he had been knocked off the perilous granite wall. He tried to maintain his grip on the wet rocks, but felt the fingernails of his left hand breaking with the impact.

Then his boots slipped off their narrow footholds.

Suddenly Slim was hanging there with only the fingers of one hand keeping him from falling into the canyon. The haunting laughter of his brother filled his ears as he watched the massive black storm clouds envelop the very peak of the mountain. The sky suddenly started rumbling again. Small white flashes of lightning darted across the heavens as if scouting for the perfect place to strike.

Gritting his teeth, Slim swung back and forth helplessly, trying to grab hold of anything to steady himself. The cowboy screwed up his eyes and watched his laughing brother continuing his ascent.

For what seemed an eternity, Slim dangled helplessly until he felt the muscles and bones of his arm screaming out in agony as they took the full weight of his body. He had to act fast if he were going to survive.

Forcing his legs to swing violently, Slim scraped at the rocks with the toe-caps of his boots seeking anything solid enough to plant them on to. Then the cowboy managed to feel one boot jamming into a small crevice no bigger than three inches wide and half as deep.

Slim took a deep breath, pressed his body into the rocks and searched for another foothold as his fingers scratched desperately above him. Slim finally found enough grip with the side of his worn heel to hold himself for a few seconds as his fingers found that elusive handhold.

Every part of him hurt. Slim was sure he had torn half the muscles in his body apart and knew that he had no chance of bridging the gap between them now.

At last, Zane had defeated him.

Resting his bleeding temple against the wet cold rocks Slim managed to calm himself and force himself upwards until he was taking his full weight on his boots.

Then, looking up, he saw that Zane had managed to reach a narrow ledge and was climbing on to it.

What came next chilled Slim to the bone.

Helplessly he watched as Zane pulled the Colt from his right holster and transferred it to his left hand. The sound of his brother's crazed laughter echoed all around Skull Canyon as he cocked the pistol's hammer and took aim.

There was only one target, and Slim Walker knew that he was it.

Forcing the toes of his cowboy boots into the small cracks of the mountain until he was able to balance, Slim bit his lip and stared up at Zane. The laughter seemed to drown out the thunder as it rumbled all about them. Slim looked past the shining gun barrel that was trained on him, and into the eyes of Zane.

It was pointless. Zane had never had a soul like other men.

Suddenly a deafening blast overwhelmed the hysterical laughter and a massive bolt of lightning splintered out of the huge black clouds and forked through the air until it found the barrel of the raised Colt .45.

Slim lowered his head as the blinding light exploded above him. A million fragments of granite showered over his shoulders as he clung to his precarious perch.

For more than five minutes the cowboy just held on to the vibrating rockface, knowing that if he moved a muscle he would be sent spiralling down into the canyon.

Slowly everything began to go quiet. When Slim eventually found the courage to look back up, his heart began to pound inside his blood-soaked shirt.

A thousand sticks of dynamite could not have taken a bigger chunk out of the granite mountainside, Slim thought.

He looked at the sky and noticed that the last of the menacing clouds had at last moved off towards the vast open ranges to the north. He could feel the warmth of the sun on his bleeding hands.

Zane was gone.

Slim Walker had won, but felt no satisfaction. It was a hollow victory.

FINALE

It had taken the three young Apaches more than an hour to reach Slim Walker and bring him carefully down into the heart of Skull Canyon.

The cowboy had said nothing for more than an hour as the sweltering heat rose ferociously. The Apaches had given him water and tended his wounds, but nothing seemed to be able to make the injured man speak. It was as if his mind had switched off in shock at what had happened high above them. Yet he felt no grief or sense of loss.

For some strange reason he knew that he had been released from a terrible curse.

Sheriff Peabody had greeted the arrival of his deputy and the two lawmen had inspected the cave. What they found hidden there made up for the loss of the reward money.

Heronis stood before the seated cowboy and placed a hand on the young man's shoulder. Slim looked up at the face of the man who had selflessly helped him.

'You good man. You should not be of heavy heart,' the chief said. 'You not kill him. The Great Spirit sent down a mighty arrow from the happy hunting ground.'

'I guess you're right, Heronis,' Slim replied getting to his feet and staring up at the mountain. 'But however evil he was, he was still my brother.'

'He had not been your brother for many moons.' Heronis pointed at the three young braves. 'These your brothers, Slim.'

The cowboy smiled and patted the grey-haired Apache's shoulder.

'A man could be mighty proud of such a family. I am.'

The pair of lawmen carried a large wooden box towards them and dropped it on the ground. It was filled with golden eagles and more paper money than any of them had ever seen before.

'We figure that there must be at least ten thousand bucks here,' Peabody said, rubbing his whiskered chin.

Slim nodded.

'That sounds about right.'

The sheriff leaned closer to the tall cowboy.

'The trouble is, I got me a problem.'

Slim touched his broken nose and tilted

his head. 'What kinda problem, Sheriff.'

'Well, there ain't no way of telling who this loot belongs to, son. We had a good look around in the cave but there weren't no bank bags or the like up there. We figure he must have burned them.'

'So?'

'We don't know whose money this is.' Peabody sighed.

Slim walked across to the black stallion and ran a hand down its neck. The animal seemed to sense he had a new master as the cowboy untied the reins and led him back to the men. The Apache had laden it down with two huge water-bags across its sturdy shoulders.

'What do we do with it?' Tom Smith asked.

Slim Walker grabbed the saddle horn, stepped into the stirrup and hauled himself on to the back of the big black horse. He sat in the saddle and thought about the question carefully. Then he stared at the four Indians before returning his attention to the sheriff and deputy.

'I figure that you boys ought to claim it. You found it, so I reckon it's yours. But it would be kinda nice if you could buy my Apache brothers some provisions and a few beef steers and maybe a milk cow.' Slim gathered up the reins in his hands. 'They got a lot of old folks and children starving up in the crags, Sheriff.'

Peabody spat a lump of black goo at the ground and then offered his hand to the cowboy.

'Me and Tom will make sure that these folks don't get any more hungry.'

Slim shook the hand and then smiled at Heronis.

'These men will bring your people food, Chief.'

'Ride safe, my brother.'

The cowboy turned the head of the fine stallion, then tapped his spurs and rode across the red sand.

He would never again return to Skull Canyon.

The publishers hope that this book has given you enjoyable reading. Large Print Books are especially designed to be as easy to see and hold as possible. If you wish a complete list of our books please ask at your local library or write directly to:

Dales Large Print Books
Magna House, Long Preston,
Skipton, North Yorkshire.
BD23 4ND

This Large Print Book, for people
who cannot read normal print,
is published under the auspices of

THE ULVERSCROFT FOUNDATION

... we hope you have enjoyed this book.
Please think for a moment about those
who have worse eyesight than you ...
and are unable to even read or enjoy
Large Print without great difficulty.

You can help them by sending a
donation, large or small, to:

**The Ulverscroft Foundation,
1, The Green, Bradgate Road,
Anstey, Leicestershire, LE7 7FU,
England.**
or request a copy of our brochure for
more details.

The Foundation will use all donations
to assist those people who are visually
impaired and need special attention
with medical research, diagnosis
and treatment.

Thank you very much for your help.